Lynn

**Evie knew sh**
**out of her c**
**probably flirt**
**the same tim**
**seem to dredge up a care.**

This was a whole new world, and it was scary and thrilling. If she had an ounce of sense she'd go back to her suite at the Bellagio and forget she'd ever laid eyes—or hands—on this man.

Embarrassed, she could only smile gratefully and hope the darkness would hide the blush on her cheeks.

"Would you like to go somewhere else? Some-place a bit quieter?"

"That sounds good to me."

Nick stood and offered her his hand. "Then let's go."

She hesitated for a millisecond, wondering out of habit what the gossip columns would make of her and Nick, but then she remembered where she was. *What happens in Vegas, stays in Vegas.* No one here knew or even gave a damn who she was, what she did, or who she did it with.

Then Nick smiled at her, and her knees wobbled.

**Viva Las Vegas!**

**Dear Reader**

Some of you may be thinking something sounds vaguely familiar about this book…and you'd be right.

When I finished writing my second book, THE MILLIONAIRE'S MISBEHAVING MISTRESS, there was one character who just wouldn't let me go: Evie. Evie was such a strong character, and I loved her so much, I actually missed her once the book was done. I chalked that up to author over-investment, and went on to other books and other characters. But I never forgot about her. Once THE MILLIONAIRE'S MISBEHAVING MISTRESS hit the shelves, I started getting e-mails and feedback from readers, and soon it became clear I wasn't the only one who'd fallen in love with her and wanted to see her safely settled with her own Happily-Ever-After.

But what to do with a character like Evie? She's rich and beautiful, and she comes from a great family, and I'd just written an entire book setting her up to do well in her life. She seemed to have a pretty clear path ahead. What could she possibly need?

I realised I'd created an irrepressible character and then done my level best to repress her in every way possible. What would happen when Evie couldn't take it any more and everything she'd been holding back exploded to the surface? I also needed to find her a hero who'd challenge her, shake her up, and appreciate who she was at her core. Nick Rocco fitted the bill nicely—a Mr Totally Wrong who turns out to be Mr Completely Perfect.

Giving Evie her hero and her Happily-Ever-After has been a joy for me, and I thank everyone who let me know how much they wanted her to have her own story. I hope you're pleased with the result.

All the best

*Kimberly*

# WHAT HAPPENS IN VEGAS…

BY
KIMBERLY LANG

First published in Great Britain 2010
Harlequin Mills & Boon Limited,
Eton House, 18-24 Paradise Road, Richmond, Surrey TW9 1SR

© Kimberly Kerr 2010

ISBN: 978 0 263 87744 1

Harlequin Mills & Boon policy is to use papers that are natural, renewable and recyclable products and made from wood grown in sustainable forests. The logging and manufacturing process conform to the legal environmental regulations of the country of origin.

Printed and bound in Spain
by Litografia Rosés, S.A., Barcelona

**Kimberly Lang** hid romance novels behind her textbooks in junior high, and even a Master's programme in English couldn't break her obsession with dashing heroes and happily ever after. A ballet dancer turned English teacher, Kimberly married an electrical engineer and turned her life into an ongoing episode of *When Dilbert Met Frasier.* She and her Darling Geek live in beautiful North Alabama, with their one Amazing Child—who, unfortunately, shows an aptitude for sports.

Visit Kimberly at www.booksbykimberly.com for the latest news—and don't forget to say hi while you're there!

**Recent titles by the same author:**

BOARDROOM RIVALS, BEDROOM FIREWORKS!
MAGNATE'S MISTRESS…
   ACCIDENTALLY PREGNANT!
THE MILLIONAIRE'S MISBEHAVING MISTRESS
THE SECRET MISTRESS ARRANGEMENT

To Shelley Visconte, MA, LPC, LMFT
and soon-to-be PhD—I'm so proud of you,
and terribly impressed by that alphabet soup behind
your name, but the letters that make me
the proudest are the ones you've had all along: BFF.

# CHAPTER ONE

THAT WAS AN ACTUAL mirrored disco ball spinning over a lighted dance floor. Hundreds of sweaty bodies crowded the dance floor, moving to a techno dance mix, and the bass line thumped like a heartbeat. This club—The Zoo—had strobe lights, LED-lit jungle vines hanging from the ceiling and zebra-striped furniture. This place took tacky to a whole new level.

And Evie Harrison loved it. In fact, she loved everything about Las Vegas: the neon lights, the over-the-top, let-it-all-hang-out attitude, the sheer unapologetic gaudiness of the entire city.

Las Vegas wasn't Dallas, that was for sure, and *that* made Evie love Vegas all the more.

"Wanna dance, gorgeous?"

Evie's eyes watered at the alcohol exhaled in her face as the offer was made. "No, but thanks. I'm waiting on someone."

Thankfully, her would-be dance partner was still in the "happy drunk" stage, and he only shrugged as he moved one table over, presumably with the same question.

The truth was, she *would* like to dance. But hitting the dance floor alone wasn't an option. Not that she cared who saw her or what they thought—the joy of anonymity was part of what brought her to Vegas in the first place—but a woman dancing alone would bring every drunk guy in the bar immediately into her personal space, and she couldn't guarantee they'd all be as easily rebuffed as the last one.

A cocktail waitress with tiger ears on her head and whiskers painted across her cheeks picked up the empty glass off the table. "Can I get you something?" she shouted over the music.

"A vodka tonic," Evie replied, as her tiny silver purse began to dance across the table from the vibration of the cell phone inside. She pulled out the phone and looked at the number displayed on the screen.

Will.

There was no way in hell she was answering that. The phone quit vibrating as the call went to voice mail, and Evie noted it wasn't the first time her brother had called tonight. A quick scroll through the missed-call log showed this was the fourth time in the last two hours Will had called. She was busted.

She'd left Will a message at his office telling him she was leaving town. He wasn't supposed to get it until Monday morning. The workaholic butthead must've checked his messages already.

She would not feel guilty. She was twenty-five years old—even if Will still thought she was a wayward teenager—and she didn't need her brother's permission to leave town for the weekend.

Her drink arrived at the same time as a text from Sabine. *Going to casino @ Bellagio with Toby. Don't wait up.* The last sentence was unnecessary; she'd recognized the look in Bennie's eyes when she'd left thirty minutes ago and known their girls' night out was officially over.

She was a little disappointed, but at least Bennie had dropped everything to come to Vegas with her last night when she asked.

And honestly, being alone in Vegas sure beat being in Dallas at the moment. Being *anywhere* beat being at home right now.

So she lost her patience and said a few things at that brunch she shouldn't have. Evie frowned into her drink. If that witch from the *Dallas Lifestyles* gossip column hadn't been standing right there minding everyone *else's* business, no one would have ever known. But *no,* the whole embarrassing thing got prime treatment on page three yesterday morning.

She'd apologized to the Dallas Beautification Committee's president *and* doubled the amount of the company's donation to make up for implying that new benches in the city's parks weren't equally as important as curing cancer or feeding the hungry.

No one reported *that* in the paper. No, they were too busy getting as much ink as possible out of her big mouth. Again. Then Will had jumped on her case about it, and she'd gotten a nice long talking-to from Uncle Marcus—*again*—about not embarrassing the family—*again*—but neither of *them* was sitting through endless brunches and endless speeches just to be the smiling face that presented a check on behalf of HarCorp International.

Why had she even bothered going to college? A trained monkey could do her job. Hell, a *well*-trained monkey might manage not to make the paper while doing so.

So what if Will was all bent out of shape that she was AWOL? It wouldn't be the first time he'd wanted to strangle her, and it probably wouldn't be the last time, either.

Her phone vibrated again. This time it was Gwen's number. Did Will honestly think she'd answer a call from his wife's phone when she wasn't taking calls from him? How dumb did he think she was?

She made a face at the phone before she tucked it back into her purse. With Bennie off with her new friend, Evie reassessed her options for the rest of the evening. She could be good and go back to the hotel, but that defeated the entire purpose of running away from home in the first place. She just needed a time-out from her life, the chance to have some fun without worrying everything she did would end up in the papers.

That ad campaign for Las Vegas claimed What Happens in Vegas, Stays in Vegas. That sounded fantastic.

It was time to go find something to do.

Whoever designed this club should be shot. It *was* possible to take a theme too far. And if they were aiming for a zoo theme, why on earth were jungle vines hanging from the ceiling?

Nick Rocco mentally tallied up how much it would cost to completely gut and refurbish the interior of The Zoo and added it to the total cost.

If he bought The Zoo—and that was still an if—he'd have to close it completely during renovations. But it was in a prime location, and a big, splashy, grand reopening might give the club a boost and added publicity. Any loss from the closure *could* be recouped if he handled the reopening properly.

Even with the added cost and delay, adding The Zoo to his collection of properties made good business sense. He'd also readily admit it gave him no small sense of satisfaction to purchase a place where he'd once mopped floors and tended bar. Even if it hadn't been called The Zoo back then.

Nick made a practice of visiting any potential purchases during business hours before making firm offers to get a true feel for their potential. And any potential problems. That's why he was here on a Friday night, trying to blend in with the clientele.

The dance floor heaved with bodies, most of the low sofas and chairs were occupied, and the waitresses and bartenders were moving at a fast clip. It wasn't packed, but it wasn't dead, either. If The Zoo could pull in this much business as is, a makeover and a fresh launch could turn it into a gold mine.

Kevin O'Brian, who handled much of the day-to-day business and promotions at all of Nick's clubs, returned from his reconnaissance mission and joined him at the bar.

"Well?" Nick shouted over the thumping bass line.

"Other than the occasional drunk-and-disorderly, the cops aren't required to come by very often. I asked around, and no one seems to be picking up tricks or selling anything this place isn't licensed for." Kevin had the kind of friendly, good-ol'-boy personality that made gathering that kind of behind-the-scenes information easy. People opened up to Kevin without any effort on his part, but Nick himself didn't have the patience—or Kevin's unassuming frat-boy looks—at his disposal. The ability to play good cop/bad cop was one of the secret weapons in their business arsenal. Kevin was a valuable asset to Nick's business—as well as his oldest friend. "You'll need to fire that DJ, though."

That got his attention; Kevin rarely weighed in on staffing issues. "Why? You think he's—"

"No. His taste in music sucks." Kevin grinned and motioned for the bartender to bring him another beer. The blonde delivered it with a smile and winked at Kevin as she pocketed the tip. "Keep her, though. I like her."

"You're assuming I'm going to make the deal."

"You know you are. I'd bet this beer you've already figured how much it's going to cost you to expand the dance floor and pull down those god-awful vines."

Nick shrugged, acknowledging nothing, but Kevin knew him too well. They'd grown up together in one of the toughest parts of Las Vegas, yet unlike so many other of their childhood friends, they'd managed to get out of the circular grind of poverty and drugs. Luck *had* been involved—he'd helped fund his first major club purchase with poker winnings—but it was their common desire to escape that past that bonded them together in the hard work of the climb out of the Vegas projects to UNLV and finally to the top of the food chain.

"So, we're done now?" In the old days, Kevin would just be gearing up, but Lottie had put a stop to his partying ways.

"Go home to your wife. I'm going to stay a little longer and see how the crowd changes after the shows let out."

"You could *try* to have some fun, you know. It wouldn't kill you. You know what they say about 'All work and no play…'"

"Keeps us in the black?" Nick challenged.

"I know the books as well as you do. You don't need another club to stay in the black. You're just buying this one because you *can.*"

"And that, my friend, *is* fun."

"You're twisted. Look around—there's a lot of pretty girls here tonight…." Kevin raised his eyebrows suggestively. "I'm sure any of them would love to help you rediscover the meaning of fun."

Nick hadn't picked up a woman in a bar in years. Hooking up with a party girl out for a good time was just asking for trouble he didn't need. "Go home."

"Gone." And he was.

Nightclubs weren't Nick's idea of a place to have a good time—possibly because he'd spent too many years working in them, ensuring everyone else did. He scanned the crowd, making plans and evaluating.

Two men seemed to be having words over a small red-headed woman's attentions. From the posturing, Nick knew exactly what was coming, and he left his spot at the bar rail.

He didn't quite make it in time. The blond-haired one pushed the other one back, causing him to stumble backward into the crowd and crash into a woman behind him. Nick reached for the woman as she fell, catching her before she hit the table.

She slammed into him, her weight landing in his arms as

her feet nearly went out from under her. Something cold sloshed down his chest as he tightened his grip and turned her away from the combatants. A second later, a burly bouncer pushed past and put himself between the men, effectively stopping the fight by virtue of size and scowl.

The scuffle ended before it really began, and the two men were escorted to the door by security with the redhead trailing behind a moment later. The speed and ease with which the bouncers handled the problem impressed Nick, and he made a mental note to be sure to keep them on staff.

Looking down at the woman sprawled in his arms, he asked, "Are you okay?" as he helped her regain her balance.

The woman pushed dark auburn hair out of her face and tugged her dress back into place, calling his attention to the length of leg exposed by a tiny silver skirt and the gentle swell of her cleavage over a black top. His body seemed to remember the feel of those breasts pressed against his chest and his skin warmed a fraction.

"I think so," she replied, before she lifted green eyes to his and smiled. "Thank you for the save."

The smile lit up her face like the Vegas strip, drawing attention to her slightly exotic bone structure and causing something in him to stir.

"Oh, my God, you're wearing my drink. I'm so sorry." Her hands were on him, brushing at his chest and sending jolts through him as they did. *Damn. What was wrong with him?*

"It's fine."

"It shouldn't stain, but I'll pay your dry…" She trailed off as he grabbed her hands and held them away from his chest. "Um…your dry-cleaning bill." She slid her hands out of his grasp and extended one to him. "I'm Evie."

"Nick." Her hand disappeared inside his larger one, but she squeezed gently.

Evie looked as if she should be gracing a stage: she was

tall and willowy, with that dark hair cascading over her shoulders, and she carried herself with grace and self-assurance. Kevin would say Evie looked "expensive"—and she did—but without that fake plastic look or the sense of entitlement that normally accompanied it. He knew all too well how to spot women like that and avoid them.

"It's very nice to meet you, Nick. And you have excellent reflexes. I never even saw that guy coming."

"It happens. Testosterone, alcohol and a pretty girl is a bad mix. A common one, but a bad one."

"So *that's* what it was about." Evie seemed to think for a minute, then she turned that electric smile back on him. "I feel like I should at least offer to buy you a drink or something."

"That's not necessary."

"But—" Evie stopped and shook her head. "Oh, I'm *so* sorry. You're probably here with somebody. I don't want to start another fight, so I'll just—" She stepped away and indicated she would leave.

Oddly enough, for someone who'd come strictly to case the joint, he was now uninterested in the club itself. Evie, on the other hand. "I'm not," he heard himself say.

Evie caught her bottom lip in her teeth, and the sparkle came back to her eyes. "Then I can buy you that drink after all."

"Isn't that my line?" A couple abandoned a zebra-striped couch in favor of the dance floor, and Nick steered Evie in that direction.

"I believe the rescu*ee* should buy the rescu*er* the drink." She sat gracefully and sighed. "At least it's a bit quieter over here. I can barely hear myself think out there."

"That's kind of the point. Most people don't come here in search of stimulating conversation."

Evie cut her eyes at him. "I guess not."

A waitress appeared almost immediately to get their order. Evie ordered a vodka tonic, and though he didn't normally drink anything stronger than water when he was working, he asked for the same.

It was slightly quieter in the corner, but Evie still had to move close to him in order to hear him. As she did, the faint spicy scent of her perfume tickled his nose. It suited her perfectly—just slightly exotic and very natural.

"So where are you from, Nick?"

It took him a second to get his mind back in the conversation. "North Las Vegas."

"Really?" Her eyes widened.

He was used to looks of pity or scorn when he revealed his less-than-blue-chip background, but Evie's reaction was unexpected. "Why do you seem so surprised?"

"Because I am. I mean, I just never thought of people actually being *from* Vegas, you know? It seems like one of those places where everyone is really from somewhere else." As Evie spoke, her hands moved animatedly—until she seemed to realize she was doing it and clasped them in her lap.

"Everyone has to grow up somewhere. What about you?"

"Dallas." There was a touch of exasperation behind the word, and her mouth twisted the tiniest bit. If he hadn't been so focused on her lips, he'd have missed it. "I'm only here for the weekend."

"Not on business, then."

"God, no. Just fun."

That phrase—practically the code word for *trouble*—should've sent him to the nearest exit, but something about Evie kept him in his seat. "On your own?"

"Oh, no, I came with a friend."

He looked around pointedly, and Evie laughed. The sound caused a physical reaction—almost as if she'd run her hands over him again.

"But my friend made a new friend, so…"

Evie was on her own tonight. The same part of his brain

that was overriding his common sense took that knowledge and ran with it. He shifted on the sofa, looking for a comfortable position as his body's physical responses took over.

Thankfully, the server returned with their drinks, shifting his attention as he reached for his wallet. Evie stayed him with a hand as she handed over a bill to the server and told her to keep the change. "Smart women don't let strange men buy their drinks in bars." She winked. "It can lead to misunderstandings later."

Evie wasn't naive. He liked that. "Then I'll get the second round."

Her eyebrows went up in challenge. "That assumes there will be a second round."

"I'm not assuming anything. Just thinking positively."

"Hmm, I've heard folks talk about the power of positive thinking. Does it work for you?" Holding her drink carefully, Evie smiled as she leaned against the sofa back and crossed those unbelievably long legs. Although the action didn't look rehearsed or intentional, it was still outrageously seductive. His imagination sprang to life, and all the reasons why he didn't pick up women in bars anymore were blotted out by the images.

"I'm positive I'm glad your friend made a new friend…."

"Leaving me to make a new friend of my own?" Evie finished.

"Exactly."

That word sent a shiver down Evie's spine and kicked her heartbeat up another notch. The power of positive thinking? Hell, she was positive she wasn't thinking straight, but she was also *very* positive there was no place on earth she'd rather be than here, with Nick's dark eyes causing her stomach to turn funny flips.

When she'd landed on him and his arms tightened around her, it felt like time stopped. The imprint of his chest against hers, the heat of his skin under the silky cotton shirt, the thump of his heartbeat seeming louder than the music. And when she'd looked up to see her rescuer…

The strobe light kept sending parts of his face into shadow, emphasizing the sharp cheekbones and the strong, square line of his jaw. Dark hair fell across his forehead, nearly covering a scar above his left eyebrow that gave him a dangerous look. She'd had to break eye contact before those eyes of his sucked her in completely and turned her to mush.

Then she'd noticed how the dampness of his shirt caused it to mold across his chest, and her hands had been on him before she realized it. The electric tingle he caused in her fingertips only intensified when he grabbed her hands, and Evie had sent up a fervent prayer of thanks that God made men that looked—and felt—like him.

Only the years Gwen had spent trying to teach her to be a lady had saved her at that moment, letting her fall back into simple conversation instead of throwing herself into his arms. Her sister-in-law would be horrified at the very *un*ladylike way Evie was flirting with Nick *now,* but someone else seemed to be inhabiting her body at the moment.

*Exactly.* Was that a challenge? A promise? Nothing at all? Evie knew she was flirting way out of her comfort zone—and probably flirting with disaster at the same time—but she couldn't seem to dredge up a care. This was a whole new world, and she felt as if she'd slipped out of a confining costume and was finally herself.

It was scary and thrilling, and if she had an ounce of sense, she'd go back to her suite at the Bellagio and forget she'd ever laid eyes—or hands—on this man.

How many times had Will accused her of not having that ounce of sense? Obviously, he was right.

"Are you saying you'd like to be my new friend?" Dear

Lord, had she really just said that? And where had that husky tone come from?

The corner of Nick's mouth twitched. "Yeah."

Oh, yeah, she was way, *way* out of her league. *Switch to small talk.* Small talk would give her a graceful retreat while she regrouped. *You can do small talk.* Maybe not, she corrected herself as no words came to mind. Flustered by, well, *everything,* she reached for her glass to help calm her nerves. The vodka burned as she swallowed, and she coughed painfully. Nick signaled the waitress and she quickly brought a glass of water over.

Embarrassed, she could only smile gratefully and hope the darkness of the club would hide the blush on her cheeks.

"Since that drink doesn't seem to be to your liking, would you like to go somewhere else? Someplace a bit quieter with better-quality vodka?"

That offer nearly caused her to choke, and the water burned worse than the vodka. She cleared her throat. "Like where?"

"There's a club not far from here—the Starlight—that I like, but the options are wide open. This is Las Vegas, Evie, anything you could ever want is available twenty-four hours a day."

Her mind went to a dozen inappropriate places—complete with visuals—before she managed to rein it back in. "That sounds good to me."

Nick stood and offered her his hand. "Then let's go."

She hesitated for a millisecond and covered by reaching for her water glass one more time. Out of habit, she immediately wondered what the gossip columns would make of her and Nick, but then she remembered where she was. *What happens in Vegas, stays in Vegas.* No one here knew or even gave a damn who she was, what she did, or whom she did it with.

She placed her hand in his and her insides turned warm and melty when his fingers closed around hers and he pulled her to her feet. Feet that weren't very steady at the moment, dancing as they were around excitement, desire and the knowledge of her freedom.

Then Nick smiled at her, and her knees wobbled.

Viva Las Vegas.

# CHAPTER TWO

EVIE KNEW SHE WASN'T DRUNK—she'd only had a couple of drinks—but she certainly felt like it. The freedom, the not-caring who was watching, the feeling of lightness—the intoxication was coming from Nick, not a bottle.

Who needed alcohol when every time she inhaled, his scent coiled through her, making her blood sing in her veins? And if there was anything more perfectly thrilling than the feel of his body pressed close to hers on the dance floor... Sweet mercy. She was about to spontaneously combust. This wasn't dancing: it was rhythmic public foreplay, and the bass line vibrating through her body was an unnecessary additional stimulant.

Oh, no, Nick was more than enough.

But something more than just her libido was awake. At this moment, she wasn't "Evangeline Harrison, heiress to half of HarCorp International." She wasn't under the lens of Dallas society's microscope. No one was judging her or expecting an appropriate level of behavior from the sister-in-law of Texas's leading etiquette expert.

She was just "Evie"—random girl-on-the-street—and *that* Evie was enjoying her time out of the Dallas fishbowl. Nick didn't know any differently, and he certainly didn't seem to care who she was when she wasn't here in Las Vegas. Not only did he have no expectations of her behavior, but he also seemed blissfully ignorant of the kinds of rules she was used to.

Drinking beer straight from the bottle? He didn't bat an eyelash. Joining the band on the stage and singing backup on her favorite song? He lifted her up there and then watched her with a fire in his eyes that had her stammering into the microphone.

Nick seemed sure of himself; he wore his rough edges with pride and did what he wanted without apology. She'd spent her entire life with the "right" boys who came from families much like hers and were members of the right country clubs. Even with a veneer of civilization, Nick was what the other girls in her debutante class had called a Bad Boy.

And she'd never wanted someone so bad so *badly*.

The music ended with a crash of cymbals, and the band announced they were taking a break. Her fingers dug into Nick's muscular shoulders in protest. *No.* She didn't want this dance to end.

Nick's hand tightened around her waist, keeping her close, and her heartbeat jumped up another notch. From the way he was staring at her, she got the feeling he felt the same way. Her mouth went dry, and she swallowed hard.

The arms holding her pulled her another fraction of an inch closer until she could feel the beat of his heart against her chest. The blood roared in her ears and everything that wasn't Nick ceased to exist.

Then his mouth landed on hers.

Oh, *yes*.

His lips were warm and firm and hungry, and they fired the hunger in her. Her hand slid over the solid muscle of his shoulder, to the nape of his neck, where she was finally able to run her fingers through the inky-black silk of his hair.

She felt, more than heard, him growl low in his throat as Nick's tongue swept into her mouth to find hers.

Then she began to burn.

The fire started low in her belly, moving down through her core until her thighs began to quiver. It spread up, causing her breasts to feel heavy and her nipples to harden against the silk of her bra.

Nick's hands cupped her head, his thumbs brushing over her cheekbones to her temples as he held her steady against the onslaught.

If she'd had any worry that the tension—the want—had been only one-sided, Nick dispelled that erroneous notion with one press of his hips against hers.

"Get a room!" someone shouted, and she broke away quickly, putting distance between them.

Oh, *no.*

The lovely heat of Nick's kiss receded as the hot flush of embarrassment rushed to her cheeks. Nick didn't seem to notice—or care—as he placed one last kiss on her temple and tilted her face back up to his.

The wry smile she saw answered her question. Nick didn't care that a crowd was watching. But he did release his hold on her waist, taking her hand and twining his fingers through hers as he led her off the dance floor.

But he didn't lead her back to the table they'd occupied earlier, winding his way instead through the crowd to the bar, where he ordered another round of drinks for them. He pressed a twenty into her hand and leaned close to her ear. "Wait for the drinks, and I'll be right back."

She didn't have a chance to question him before he disappeared into the crowd. A couple of minutes later, she saw him in the back corner, next to a staircase, talking to a burly bouncer with arms the size of Texas. The bouncer nodded, and Nick headed back in her direction as the bartender set their drinks in front of her.

"What was that about?" she asked, as Nick handed her a drink, took her other hand and picked up his own glass.

"You'll see."

They approached the stairs and the bouncer standing there looked rather ferocious from up close. Without saying anything, he reached behind him, unhooked a velvet rope and waved them past.

The noise of the bar receded as they climbed the stairs to the second floor and walked down a dimly lit corridor past several closed doors. Nick finally stopped in front of one marked simply Six.

The door swung open easily, and curious, Evie stepped inside. A large window covered one wall, giving an unobstructed view of the stage and dance floor from above, and two leather-covered sofas were arranged in front of it. It was a small, intimate room with low lighting.

And privacy.

Her heart skipped a beat and she moved to the window. "This is one of those VIP rooms, isn't it?"

Nick nodded as he closed the door behind him. Evie heard it snick into place, and the muscles in her thighs tightened.

"It is—a small one, though. Usually they're a bit bigger. This one is designed for small business meetings as opposed to parties." The thick carpeting muffled his footsteps as he moved across the room toward her.

"And we managed to get it how?" Forming words was very difficult, and she was pleased she wasn't stuttering.

"I know the bouncer minding the rope. Dave owes me a favor, and since this room wasn't being used at the moment…"

*Wow.* They'd been told to get a room and now they had one. Evangeline Harrison—the one who went to nice dinners at the Club and smiled her way through cocktail-party fundraisers—reeled in shock. The Evie she'd rediscovered tonight shivered at the possibilities.

"That panel to your left controls the speakers—you'll be able to hear the band once they start up again."

*Who cared about the stupid band?*

"And that—" he pointed to what looked like a key fob to a luxury car on the table "—signals for a server. They won't enter unless you call for them."

Nick was only an arm's length away, and his intent was obvious. But he didn't take the last step that would close the gap. She guessed he was leaving that up to her. Suddenly, she felt gauche and naive and unsure of herself. "Wow, they think of everything."

Her hands were starting to tremble from the proximity and the need to touch him, and her drink sloshed over the rim. Nick held out his hand, and she handed him the glass. He set it on the table and held his hand out again.

There was a clear path to the door. She could push a button and have someone in here in just another minute.

It was her choice.

This time she placed her hand in his and welcomed the electricity that arced through her. One small step, and those strong arms closed around her, and the fire in her belly pulled the oxygen from her lungs. She required no encouragement at all to pull his head down to hers.

That hunger she'd felt earlier roared back to life full force, causing her to sway dangerously on her feet, and Nick's arms tightened, steadying her.

One hot kiss melded into another as her greedy hands traced over the contours of his back, learning the musculature. Nick's hands massaged the small of her back, sliding under the hem of her shirt to scorch her skin as his lips slid down her neck and his tongue dipped into the hollow behind her collarbone.

How they covered the short distance to the couch, she didn't know, but then Nick was easing her down and moving over her.

Evie wanted to cry at the exquisite sensation of Nick's

body on hers, the heavy weight of him settling between her legs. The cool leather of the couch was such a contrast to the scorching heat of his skin. This was heaven; this was bliss and she wanted more. She wanted all of him.

*Now.*

A push and a tug and Nick was upright on the couch, and he helped settle her onto his lap with a lazy, appreciative smile. With her legs on either side of his strong thighs and her knees snugged up next to his hips, she pressed against the bulge in his pants and gasped as a bolt of heat shot though her.

It was easy to push his shirt up and over his head, baring sculpted bronze skin to her eager hands. The dusting of crisp black hair tickled her fingers as she explored the lines and planes of his chest, and she felt the muscles jump when she brushed her thumbs over his nipples.

She was shocking herself with her actions, but not Nick. His hungry look told her that much. Again she sent up a word of thanks for Las Vegas and men like Nick. Nick was unlike any of the men at home—they were too polished, too urbane, too domesticated. Nick's rough edges excited her, made her feel as if she was dealing with something powerful and raw and untamed. It reached inside her, past the years of behaving herself, and released her.

More importantly, Nick seemed to like that part of her. Encourage it, even. It was a heady combination—the power and the freedom—and it frightened her a bit with its intensity.

Nick's hands locked around her arms, pulling her down for another soul-stealing kiss. A moment later, she felt the straps at her shoulders give way. Then the zipper of her skirt. The fabric bunched under his hands as they made their way up her body with excruciating slowness. She lifted her arms and Nick pulled both items over her head, and she fought back a blush as his eyes moved appreciatively over her body.

His fingers brushed over the top of her lacy strapless bra, teasing her nipples and causing her thighs to clench. A quick twist of the clasp and it joined the rest of her clothes on the ground.

She hissed as Nick's tongue snaked out to tease, then bit back a cry when he pulled her aching nipple into the moist heat of his mouth. His hands went to her waist, pressing down as he lifted his hips and pressed against her very needy core.

Oh, *yesss.*

A tug on his hair and Nick was kissing her again, his tongue sliding across hers in a way that made her insides melt and her breathing ragged. His hands cupped her face gently as she worked on his belt and slid his zipper down.

She caught his groan in her mouth as she palmed him, running her hand over the hard length of an impressive erection that made her shiver with anticipation. Nick's eyes closed and he leaned back, his fingers digging into her thighs as she stroked him. Evie felt powerful, sexy, pleased she could make Nick feel even a part of that burning ache he stoked in her.

Nick suddenly surged forward, capturing her mouth in a savage kiss as he lifted her to the side easily with only one arm, using the other to slide her panties down her legs and off. That same dexterity had the rest of his clothes off in a blink, and he settled her back into her original position.

With a bravado she didn't know she had, she managed to meet his eyes and hold the stare as he tickled his fingers along her inner thigh, teasing her before his thumb slipped between her damp folds and wrung a moan from her with barely a touch.

Nick cursed, and holding her in place, leaned forward and reached for the table. Confused, she turned her head in time to see him slide open a drawer. Condoms filled the small space.

*They weren't the first people to use this room for...* She tried to swallow her shock. "Oh. Goodness."

"These rooms are for private parties, too."

*Of course they are.* Nick must think she was some kind of naive country girl. She tried to sound airy and sophisticated. "They really do think of everything here, don't they?"

Nick's smile caught her off guard. "Thank God they do."

She couldn't argue with that, and she was thankful Nick was coherent enough to remember the basics. Her brain had definitely checked out. Nick placed the condom on the cushion next to him and settled back into place.

In no rush, his hands began exploring her body again, teasing her nipples, sliding a strong finger inside her until her nails were digging into his biceps and she was gasping for breath.

An eternity later, she heard the beautiful sound of a condom packet being ripped open, and Nick was guiding her hips into position.

Evie couldn't stifle her groan of pleasure as she sank slowly onto him, savoring each centimeter until they were completely locked together. Her thighs shook as she started to move, Nick's hands helping her set the pace.

Sweet *mercy,* she was going to die, right here, from the sheer bliss of the feel of him in her. She let her forehead fall against his as the movement became more frantic, the pleasure sharper and more intense. She felt light-headed as the pressure built, radiating out until her entire body began to shake, and she threw her head back and screamed his name as she shattered into a thousand glittering pieces.

He'd never used one of his VIP lounges for sex before. He'd hosted a small gathering in this room only once: last year when they'd celebrated the purchase of the Starlight. He had good memories of that night, but tonight guaranteed he'd never look at this room the same way again. Every piece of furniture, the floor, even the long wall of windows, would now hold the image of Evie, naked and panting and crying out his name.

Evie lay back against the couch, her hair a tangle of curls cascading over the edge to nearly touch the carpet. The picture she created was more than enough to get his blood pumping again, although it shouldn't be possible after he'd taken her so many times he'd lost count. But the band had long ago called it quits for the night, and the slowdown on the dance floor told him how late it was. He checked his watch to be sure.

He ran a hand over the leg Evie had draped across his lap, and she sighed contentedly. "Starlight closes at four. We should probably get dressed."

Evie switched from sensual to shy in a heartbeat; the woman who'd clawed his back and screamed his name—repeatedly—couldn't seem to meet his eyes now. A blush stained her cheeks as modesty returned about three hours too late, and she fumbled for her clothes.

"Um, okay…sure. Just give me a minute."

Her face was redder than the desert sunset, and she practically ran for the attached bathroom, giving him a lovely view of her backside as she retreated.

He untangled his own clothes and pulled his shirt on over his head, surprised to find that the scent of Evie's perfume clung faintly to it. The smell wasn't a familiar one—he couldn't place it. It was heady, yet subtle, exotic and unique.

Much like Evie.

She was tempting and seductive, yet there was a wholesome genuineness underneath. She seemed cautious to approach new things—even hesitant at times—but she had an adventurous streak that couldn't be denied. Her honeyed Texas drawl wasn't affected, but it gave way sometimes to something else, leading him to believe she wasn't a true Dallas native.

Part of him thought she had to be from that Southern aristocracy he'd heard about; she had class, elegance and she could be unbelievably polite and well-mannered. At the same time, she lacked that air of superiority Old-Money people had: that belief they were somehow better than everyone else just because great-grandpa once owned half the town.

He had personal experience with Old Money and New Money. Vegas was full of New-Money people—hell, he was one of them—and he far preferred the New Money over the Old, even if he was, technically, *biologically* at least, both.

Evie returned—dressed, hair somewhat tamed—but still looking as if she'd been…well, having sex for the last four hours. Her lips were slightly swollen, and her jaw was a little red from where his stubble had rubbed.

Still not quite able to make eye contact, Evie retrieved her shoes from under the table and grabbed her purse. "I'm ready," she claimed, as she hurried to slide her feet into the strappy silver sandals.

"Don't rush. No one's going to be banging down the door."

"Well, I don't want Dave to get in trouble for letting us up here."

He bit back a smile at that.

"Here. Take these." She pushed glassware into his hands and started straightening the cushions on the couch.

"You don't have to do that, Evie."

"If this room wasn't supposed to be used tonight, they'll know someone was up here when they see the mess."

"Don't worry about it."

Evie frowned. "Nick…"

With no way to explain that wouldn't tell her more about his finances than he wanted her to know, he bit his tongue and took the empty glasses.

Evie *had* to notice the number of strange looks sent their way as they came down the stairs. Earlier, when the place had been hopping, only a few people had noticed he was here. Now, with so few customers still hanging on, he could see the questions on every face of the Starlight staff.

Evie's cheeks grew redder and redder and her feet moved faster, until she was out the door in almost a full trot. Outside, she leaned against a wall and covered her face with her hands. "Oh, my *God,* that was so embarrassing."

"What?"

"Did you not see everyone staring at us? I felt like I was carrying a giant neon sign that said We Just Had Sex."

He laughed, but smothered it with a cough when Evie turned stormy eyes on him. "It's not funny."

"You don't know these people, and you'll never see them again, so why do you care?"

Evie leaned her head back against the concrete wall. "I guess you're right. That only makes it *slightly* less embarrassing."

He'd never seen anyone die of embarrassment before, but Evie had to be close, so he took pity on her, even though he was loath to end their evening. "It's late, and I have to work in the morning. I'll take you back to your hotel. Where are you staying?"

"The Bellagio." Her voice sounded small and he wondered why.

A taxi coasted to a stop, and he opened the door for Evie to climb in. In the backseat, Evie seemed even more withdrawn, a huge change from her brightness earlier. Unable to ask why when the cabbie was listening, he settled for lame small talk. "That's a nice hotel. Have you had a chance to explore it?"

"Not really. Bennie—Sabine," she corrected, "and I did a little shopping earlier today."

"Bennie's the friend who came with you?"

Evie nodded. "But I haven't been to the casino yet. I'm not much of a gambler."

"Don't like it?"

"Don't know how to play any of the games. I've played penny-ante poker with my brother and blackjack on my laptop, but that's about it."

"I could teach you." Why had he offered that? He hadn't been in a casino in years.

"You'd do that?" Evie brightened considerably. Maybe she really did want to learn to gamble.

"If you'd like."

Her mood improved exponentially at that point, and by the time they pulled in at the Bellagio, Evie was almost back to her earlier self.

Including using her best manners. "I had a great time tonight, Nick. Thank you."

"My pleasure." *Understatement of the year.*

A Bellagio doorman opened the taxi door, and Nick slid out and extended a hand to Evie. Once she was on her feet, he slid a hand under her chin and turned her face up for a kiss.

Evie's response was as voracious as before, and he let the kiss continue until the cabbie started complaining about the wait. Evie stepped back, another adorable blush rising over her cleavage.

"Do you know the bar that overlooks the fountain?"

She nodded.

"Meet me there at seven tonight."

Evie's smile could be breathtaking, especially when she rose up on her tiptoes to kiss him one last time before finally turning to the doorman patiently holding the lobby door open.

At the door, she turned and waved.

He directed the cabbie to take him back to The Zoo, where he had left his car in a not-great alley off a side street. At the time, he only planned to be in the club for a couple of hours, tops. If he'd known it would be more like six, he'd have found a safer spot. Hopefully, it would still have a stereo and all four tires when he returned.

Hell, who was he kidding? He didn't care, even as he noticed the broken window. A night with Evie was well worth the consequences.

# CHAPTER THREE

EVIE FELT LIKE SKIPPING through the Bellagio lobby, but ladies didn't skip through hotel lobbies. She stamped down the urge.

She'd just had what was possibly the best night of her entire life, and even better, Nick wanted to do it *again* tonight. Ladylike or not, *that* thought put a bounce in her step anyway.

Even at this time of the night—or technically, morning— the lobby was active, the employees greeting her politely as if she didn't look as if she'd just come in after a night of debauchery. She should feel exposed and embarrassed, since it was obvious what she'd been up to, but she realized that probably wasn't an uncommon occurrence in Las Vegas.

And, as Nick had reminded her, it's not as if she'd ever see these people again.

In the elevator, she slipped out of her shoes and stretched tiredly. The adrenaline and endorphin rush she'd been on all night dissipated quickly now that Nick wasn't around to fuel it, and exhaustion settled heavily on her shoulders. An enormous yawn cracked her jaw, and she really, really needed to sleep.

She closed the door to the suite behind her quietly. Sabine's shoes and evening bag were on the couch, and the door to her room was shut. Evie had no way of knowing if Bennie was alone in there or not.

And to be honest, she was too tired to care.

Evie collapsed on her bed and stared at the ceiling. She was keyed up mentally, sated physically and totally exhausted. She should shower, maybe eat something, but her legs felt too heavy to move. Getting out of her clothes almost sounded like far too much work, but she managed to shimmy out of them and wrap a robe around herself before she pushed the button to close the drapes and crawled under the covers.

When she closed her eyes, Nick's face was there. She could feel the imprint of his hands on her hips, taste him on her lips, hear that low growl. She wanted to relive every moment and savor the anticipation of tonight, but sleep was dragging her under quickly….

"Jeez, Evie, wake up. How hungover are you?"

Evie felt Sabine land on her bed next to her. "I'm not hungover. Just tired," she mumbled. "Go 'way."

"The day is half-over, and I still haven't heard about your night. What time did you get in, anyway?"

"Dunno. Four-ish. Maybe?" She pulled the pillow over her head as Bennie pushed the button controlling the drapes and light flooded the room. "Late."

"Way to go, Evie! I want details. Graphic ones." Sabine shook her shoulder. "Spare nothing."

Evie pried open her eyes and looked at the clock. After ten. "You lie. The day is not half-over. Wake me in another couple of hours." She could go back to the dream where she and Nick were swimming in that cove not far from where she grew up on St. Kitts….

"Evie Harrison, I am *dying* for details." Another shake. "Get up or I'll call Will and tell him you stayed out all night."

She didn't believe Bennie would do such a horrible thing, but… "Fine. I'm up." She untangled herself from the covers and sat up slowly.

Sabine giggled as Evie pushed her hair out of her faced and yawned. "You look awful."

Bennie, as always, looked like one of Botticelli's angels: adorable round face, curly blond hair, big blue eyes. Petite, thin and perky, Bennie was the perfect debutante. On the outside, at least. On the inside, she was more trouble than a biker gang at a Sunday School picnic. Sabine—unbeknownst to her family—was what Uncle Marcus would call a Bad Influence. It was why they were such good friends. "Thanks, Bennie. Just what I needed to hear. I feel awful, too."

Sabine handed her a bottle of water and eyed her critically. "Good thing I made reservations at the spa. It'll take them all afternoon just to take care of those bags under your eyes."

"Oh, that sounds excellent." Evie unscrewed the lid and drank deeply. Some of the cobwebs left her mind, and she felt better almost immediately. Nick had warned her that the desert air would dehydrate her. "How was your night? You and Toby have a good time? His name *was* Toby, right?"

Bennie smiled angelically. "What Toby lacks in finesse, he more than makes up for in enthusiasm and stamina. He's not the sharpest tool in the shed, but who needs conversation, anyway?" Bennie nudged her. "If I want to talk, I'll call you."

Evie scrubbed a hand over her face as she laughed. "I'm glad you had a good time."

"I *am* a little achy this morning." Rolling onto her back, Bennie stretched, then grinned. "But enough about me. I want to know who *you* hooked up with. I nearly died when I saw your text, and then when I beat you back to the room, I couldn't believe it. Spill."

"His name's Nick." A little smile tugged at her mouth.

Bennie nearly crowed. "I know that smile. Was he that good-looking or just that good?"

"Both. Tall, dark, drop-dead-oh-my-God *gorgeous*. Broad

shoulders. Great arms, too." Evie sighed, feeling like a school-girl with a crush.

Bennie echoed her sigh. "Oh, I love good arms."

"I had a fabulous time, though." Evie scooted to the head of the bed and leaned against the headboard.

"I can tell."

"Not just *that*." She tried for a disapproving frown, but Bennie laughed it off. "Well, the sex *was* fabulous, too, but we danced and talked—"

"Why on *earth* would you waste time talking if he was that hot?"

"Because I like to get to know people a little bit before I get naked with them."

Bennie shrugged.

"So much fun and absolutely no pressure at all to do anything except enjoy myself. Have I mentioned how much I love this town?"

"I would, too, if I'd hooked up with a hottie like your Nick. Are you going to see him again?"

She could feel the goofy smile tugging at her cheeks. "He wants to do something again tonight. If you have other plans, that is. Are you seeing Toby again?"

"Lord, honey, even if I wasn't, I'd expect you to go with Nick. That's why you came here, after all."

Evie felt her jaw drop. "You think I came to Vegas just to hook up?"

Sabine was wide-eyed. "Didn't you?"

"It wasn't my primary agenda, no. I wanted to let off a little steam, drink a little, let my hair down and dance." She raised an eyebrow at Bennie. "*I* came to Vegas to have a girls' weekend."

"Then I misunderstood. My bad." Bennie was wonderfully unrepentant. "But now you've found someone yummy, so you should make the most of it. And take a few pictures tonight. I wanna see this god who's got your libido doing the lambada."

"I'll try," she promised and her stomach growled. She pounced on the distraction eagerly, not really sure she wanted to go into too much more detail with Bennie at this point. She wanted to hug it all to herself for a little while longer. "I'm starved. Is there anything in the minibar besides pretzels?"

"I took the liberty of ordering brunch. If you can hang on a little longer without falling away to a shadow, it should be here about another twenty minutes or so." Bennie gave her a once-over. "I'd recommend you use that time to grab a shower and sort out your hair. You really do look a mess."

"I do not!"

Sabine merely raised an eyebrow. "Our first appointment is at twelve-fifteen. I've booked the works—massage, mani-cure, pedicure, facial and a detoxifying hydrotherapy bath. What time are you meeting him?"

"Seven." Her pulse kicked up at the thought.

"What are you wearing?"

Damn, she had no idea what Nick had planned. "Not a clue."

"Then we'd better get moving. We may have to shop."

"You are an angel, Bennie." Evie leaned over and kissed her cheek. "What would I do without you?"

"Based solely on today? Sleep all day, starve and be cel-ibate and inappropriately dressed." Sabine threw her legs over the side of the bed and started to leave. In the doorway, she paused and turned around. "Hmm, I think I'll call the spa back and add a wax for you." She winked.

In the shower, Evie debated whether she should go tonight. Last night had just *happened.* The stars or whatever aligned to give her one wonderful night, and she should just leave it at that—a perfect memory. What if tonight didn't turn out, as well…? Who was she kidding? Tonight would be just as good as last night.

Although she would like to have a bed this time. She had a bit of a crick in her neck from last night.

She didn't even sound like herself. Standing here planning to… This wasn't like her at all. There was her usual life, and then there was…

Then there was Nick.

Bennie was right. She'd needed this. Needed someone like Nick to shake her up a little. Las Vegas had to be the next best thing to heaven.

Evie turned the tap off. Sabine must've been listening for the water to stop, because a second later, her voice drifted through the open door. "Food's here. And your phone was ringing."

Evie wrapped her hair in a towel and pulled a robe around her. Sabine was already at the table, munching on a bagel, and Evie's stomach growled. Grabbing a muffin, she took a hungry bite as she picked up her phone. Three missed calls and three messages: the first one time-stamped at eight this morning.

And every one of them was from her brother.

Damn.

The mystery and memory of Evie—and her unbelievably long legs—had haunted Nick in the four hours of sleep he'd managed to get last night before Kevin and business forced him out of bed.

By the time lunch rolled around, he'd almost convinced himself that Evie hadn't been real. Or at least not as he remembered. Beautiful women were a dime a dozen in Las Vegas; tourists out for a good time were even more plentiful. Evie was just one in a crowd—maybe he'd built more into it simply because he'd been so immersed in business he had, as Kevin insisted, gotten jaded and forgotten how to have plain ol' fun.

But that rational knowledge didn't stop him from spending way too much time deciding on a plan for tonight. He could call in a favor, get seats to the best shows or a table at the most exclusive restaurant, but he didn't want to try to impress Evie like that. He liked not having a woman know how much his bank account was worth—it tended to skew the genuineness of their reactions. And after last night, he knew that wasn't really what Evie liked anyway. She had simple tastes and didn't need ostentatious displays to have a good time.

Since he didn't want to waste all that time at shows and restaurants anyway... That gave him the perfect idea.

Kevin was in the offices at Blue—the first club Nick had purchased outright and, for sentimental reasons, still the main hub—when Nick called. And while Kevin had a mouthful of things to say about it, Nick knew it would be done.

And when Evie turned out to be less than he remembered? He shrugged. They'd still have a good time, and he'd go easily back to normalcy tomorrow.

At just a minute after seven, Nick was on the Bellagio patio watching the door while everyone else watched the fountains do their thing. When Evie walked in, nervously chewing on her bottom lip, he felt as if all the oxygen had been sucked out of his lungs.

A shimmery green dress hugged those luscious curves he'd memorized last night, the neckline plunged to reveal generous cleavage, and the hem stopped high enough to showcase her long legs. She'd piled her hair up on her head, exposing the line of her neck and emphasizing her bone structure.

If anything, his memory of last night couldn't compete with the reality.

She scanned the crowd, and when her eyes met his, she smiled shyly—at complete odds with the sensual picture she created. He wanted to meet her halfway, but his feet seemed rooted to the floor.

Then he noticed the attention she was garnering from several other places in the bar—one man was even on his feet and headed in her direction—and that kicked him into motion, a need to claim her taking hold.

"God, you're beautiful," he muttered as Evie turned her face up to his.

"I didn't know if you'd actually come tonight or not."

"How could you possibly doubt that?" He inhaled deeply and her scent shot through his veins, sending all of his blood south. They were in a hotel, for God's sake; he could have a room and have her in it in less than five minutes.

And that seemed like far too long to wait.

Evie smoothed a hand along his arm, scorching him with her touch. "You look nice." Her hand moved to his jaw. "You shaved. I kind of miss the sexy stubble."

She was killing him.

"Should we get a table?" she asked, looking around.

That brought him back to the conversation. "No. I've got a surprise for you."

Evie's eyes lit up. "A surprise? What kind of surprise?"

"If I told you, then it wouldn't be a surprise, would it?"

Evie brushed at her dress. "Is what I'm wearing okay for this surprise? I wasn't sure about the dress code…."

That scrap of fabric barely counted as a complete dress, and he was already imagining peeling it off of her. "Like I said, you look beautiful. Let's go."

Evie's heels clicked against the floor of the lobby, reminding him to slow down. He wasn't an animal dragging Evie off to mate—regardless of what his instincts were urging him to do. He could at least attempt civilized conversation. "What did you do today?"

"Slept late, hung out with Bennie. You?"

"Got up early, went to work."

"Ouch. Sorry."

Even the valet gawked at Evie as he returned with the car, but a frown from Nick put a stop to it. Evie didn't seem to notice that attention any more than she'd noticed the men in the bar. She was a danger to herself and others if she really didn't know the effect she had on men. But how could she not? Beautiful women knew they were beautiful, knew what it could do for them.

It only took a few minutes to get to Blue, and Evie looked around eagerly as he pulled into the parking lot. "Blue. Is it a nightclub? Are we going dancing again?"

He flashed back on the memory of Evie moving against him on the dance floor and groaned. That would kill him for sure. "Patience."

"Sorry. I know it's rude to ask so many questions. I'll be good."

That promise brought a visual he really didn't need at the moment, and he quickly opened the door before he mauled her in the parking lot. The hand Evie tucked under his arm caressed his bicep as if they were truly lovers, and he wondered if she was intentionally trying to drive him insane.

Blue was almost deserted at this early hour, which was fine by him. The bouncers merely nodded as he and Evie passed and the bartenders waved.

"Everyone seems to know you," Evie said.

"I know the owner, so I'm here a lot." He led her past a velvet rope and down the back hallway.

"I don't think we're supposed to be back here," Evie whispered as she tugged against his hand.

At the elevator, he pulled her close. "I told you, I know the owner. Don't worry."

She looked around, clearly unconvinced. "Is there anyone in Vegas you don't know or who doesn't owe you a favor?"

"I've lived here a long time, Evie."

"I do *not* want to get arrested in Las Vegas." Her eyes narrowed as the elevator doors opened, and she stared pointedly at the sign marked Private.

"You're not going to get arrested. I promise." Evie still looked suspicious. "I thought you'd like to do something a bit different, so I made a couple of calls this afternoon. Look," he added as the doors opened onto the roof.

Evie gasped. Facing west, they had a great view of the sun starting to set.

"Later in the summer it gets too hot to be up here at this time, but it's about perfect now." And he wasn't just referring to the weather.

"It's gorgeous," Evie said as she crossed to the chest-high wall that enclosed the patio. "Is this another VIP-type room?"

"Sort of." Blue's rooftop was very exclusive, but Evie had no way of knowing that. He'd hired one of the best designers in Las Vegas to create an oasis here: plenty of green plants, indirect lighting, low couches canopied with gauzy fabrics, small fountains. A giant shade stretched overhead to keep the worst of the sun off, but also gave the roof an intimate feel. Kevin called it the Sheik's Tent.

"This is…wow."

He agreed. Evie looked fabulous backlit by the sunset—she seemed to glow. She moved away from the edge to run a hand along the back of a chaise, then moved to examine the table set for two.

She raised an eyebrow as he lifted the champagne out of its bucket. "A private party?"

"Only a very select guest list."

A smile tugged at the corners of Evie's mouth. "Be sure and thank the owner for me. This is absolutely perfect." Before he could respond, Evie was pressed against him, her hands sliding to his shoulders as she rose up on her toes. "The elevator is locked? All the guests are here?"

He slid his fingers into her hair and found the combs holding it up. One small tug and it tumbled around her shoulders. "Uh-huh."

"Good." Then Evie's mouth met his.

The want that had slowly simmered in his veins all day boiled over in that instant, and his hands tightened in her hair to hold her. Evie's fingers gripped his shoulders, and her nails stabbed against his skin when his mouth moved to the column of her neck and her head dropped back to allow him better access.

She sighed, then shivered, as he tasted her, and the shiver moved through him, as well. Nimble fingers made quick work of the buttons on his shirt, and she slid her hands across his bare chest before she wrapped her arms around him and pressed herself against him again.

Evie's height had their bodies aligned perfectly—her breasts rubbed against his chest and he felt the hard points of her nipples through the thin material of her dress.

He walked backward, pulling Evie with him, until he felt the edge of the couch butt against his calves. Evie groaned in protest as he broke the kiss to lower her down, her hands fisting in his shirt to pull him down to join her.

Déjà vu. Only better.

Maybe Kevin was on to something calling the roof the Sheik's Tent. Nick certainly felt like the Sultan of Something, lying on a couch with a mostly naked Evie draped across him as they nibbled on fruit and cheese and watched the city lights cause the sky to glow.

Evie's bag started to ring, and she wrinkled her nose. But she didn't move beyond examining another strawberry.

"Aren't you going to get that?"

"Not just no, *hell* no." She picked up her champagne flute and drank deeply.

He'd never met a woman who could resist a phone. "Why not?"

"That's my brother's ringtone. And I am *not* in the mood to deal with my butthead of a brother."

It was the first time she'd mentioned anyone in her family specifically. "Family problems?"

"Yeah. No. Sort of." She sighed and pushed her hair back from her face. "I left town without telling him, and he's a bit peeved about it. He's left me several voice mails this weekend telling me exactly how much."

"Your *brother* is upset you left town?"

"My parents died when I was young. Will and Gwen—she's his wife—took me in and raised me. So Will treats me rather like a child."

"And you're dodging his calls? No offense, but isn't that a little childish?"

Evie smacked him playfully. "You don't know my brother."

"As you said, you are an adult. What could he possibly do to you?"

"Nothing but yell at me, but that's never stopped him before. Will's just… He's a…" She sat up and pulled his shirt closed around her. "Something happened earlier this week—nothing major—but it got blown a bit out of proportion. He got mad, and I got mad and now I'm AWOL because I wanted a *break* from the drama. I certainly don't want to hear it while I'm here." She sighed and grimaced. "Will thinks he's the master of the whole freakin' universe and, therefore, in charge of everything."

"Including you."

Evie rolled her eyes. "Definitely including me. I know he means well, but, dear God, it gets old. It got old about the time I turned twenty-one. Do you have any siblings?"

"No." *Thank God.* It was tough enough getting himself out, if he'd had to worry about siblings, too… "It was just me and my father after my mother left."

Evie's eyes clouded. "Your mom left?"

He stiffened at the question. He very rarely spoke of his

mother, and those that knew the story had learned long ago not to broach the subject. He couldn't fault Evie for asking since he'd brought it up, but he was surprised at himself that he'd let it slip out.

Evie blanched. "I'm sorry. That was terribly rude of me to ask such a personal question. Please don't feel like you owe me any response at all. Forget I said anything."

She seemed so sincere, he almost wished he could explain. "No apology necessary, Evie. I just don't like to talk about it."

"Why don't we just *not* talk about our families? Everyone has some nuts on the family tree—some are just more annoying than others."

"And some think they're the master of the universe."

"Indeed. He'll have plenty of opportunity to yell at me tomorrow when I get home. Why settle for the telephone version when the live action is *so* much more interesting."

It seemed Evie had an interesting family dynamic. But they'd called a halt to all uncomfortable family discussions, so he didn't press the topic.

"It's a shame you have to go back so quickly."

Evie shrugged as she settled her head against his chest and traced circles on his skin. "But if I ever make it back to Vegas…"

"Give me a call," he finished.

She pressed a kiss on his chest and he responded by rolling her to her back and settling his body between her legs. Evie looked adorably mussed—hair tangled from his hands, mouth slightly swollen—and sexy as hell. He rested his chin on her chest, enjoying the silky feel of her skin as she toyed with his hair.

Evie ran her thumb over his eyebrow, and he knew what was coming next. "How'd you get this scar?"

"Bar fight."

She laughed, causing her body to move under his in a way guaranteed to get his attention. "No, seriously."

"I am serious. A guy swung a bottle, and I got this."

"Oh, my gosh, I've never met anyone who's even witnessed a bar fight, much less been in one." She looked at him oddly. "Who started it? Was it over a girl? Like last night at The Zoo?"

"I wasn't *in* the fight, Evie, I was trying to break it up." Understanding crossed her face, and she nodded. "It was part of my job—breaking up fights, that is. I was working at this sleazy joint when I was in high school—"

Evie's eyes went wide. "High school? Isn't that a little bit illegal?"

"Maybe. But I needed a job and Henry—the owner—needed a bar back and someone to help break up fights."

"The fights were a regular occurrence?"

"I told you, testosterone and alcohol are a dangerous mix." She grinned. "What about the pretty girl?"

"Not always necessary—especially in sleazy joints."

"Were you this big in high school?" She ran her hands over his shoulders as she asked, and the openly appreciative look on her face caused his body to harden again.

"About."

Evie's hands were now on his arms, tracing his biceps. "Linebacker for the football team?"

He could have been, had he not had to work. "Nope."

"Let me guess, between your size and your scowl, you're good at breaking up bar fights."

To the best of his knowledge, he hadn't scowled since Evie landed in his arms last night. That had to be a world record—but Evie didn't know that. "What makes you think I scowl?"

She ran a finger across his forehead. "This crease here. Definitely caused by scowling." Evie trailed her finger down over his cheek and to his lips. "Who do you scowl at now?"

"Drunks in bars. Such is the hospitality industry in Las Vegas." He captured her finger between his lips and sucked gently. Under his chin, he felt her heartbeat accelerate.

"So that's how you know the owner of this place—and everyone else." She smirked. "Well, you certainly are hospitable."

He nipped at her finger, causing her to jump. He pushed himself up, wedging his hips firmly between hers, and caught her gasp in his mouth.

Evie's hands slid up his back as her tongue slipped inside his mouth to torment him. She echoed his groan as his hands tangled in her hair, and her legs wrapped around his waist.

Faintly, he heard her phone ring again.

# CHAPTER FOUR

EVIE PACED WHILE THE TIMER counted down the last few seconds. The cool blues and greens of her apartment decor were supposed to create a soothing and relaxing environment. They were failing miserably.

When the timer dinged, she jumped. "Please, please, please," she mumbled as she walked through to her bathroom—also done in soothing colors and also falling down on the job.

She looked carefully at the array of tests lined up on the vanity. Six different brands, purchased at four different stores in the next county this morning after she'd called in sick to the office.

Every last one of the damn things said "positive."

Oh, she really felt sick now. She sat on the edge of the tub while the horrid reality settled on her shoulders.

Last night, she'd turned the calendar over to June and realized she hadn't had a period in May. That thought lead her to her day planner, where she realized she last had her period the week before she went to Las Vegas.

Sleep was impossible after that.

But she'd kept calm—sort of—telling herself there was no need to panic until she had a reason to. She looked at the line of tests. Oh, she had reason to panic now. Good reason.

She was pregnant.

She was going to be a mother, and, dear God, she wasn't ready to be someone's mother. She wanted children—several, in fact—but motherhood had always seemed like a distant prospect. Motherhood would come after she'd built some kind of career for herself, when she could have a house in the suburbs and do the whole nuclear-family thing with a white picket fence and a dog. And, most importantly, a husband.

Instead, she would be raising a baby alone. Well, not alone, exactly—she *did* have family—but it wouldn't have a father. How would she tell her child one day, "Your dad? Well, honey, I met him in a bar in Las Vegas…."

The child wasn't even born yet and she needed to start looking for a good therapist to help it through the issues of growing up without a father because its mother was stupid enough to get pregnant during a two-night stand in Vegas.

She ran her hands through her hair and pulled at it. "I'm so screwed. *This* is so screwed."

And it would only get worse from here. This news would kill Uncle Marcus. His heart wasn't very strong these days, and the shock and horror would kill him for sure. Pain throbbed behind her left eye. Of course, the upside was that Will was going to kill her anyway, so she wouldn't have to live with *that* guilt on her conscience for very long.

Oh, and the papers were going to have a field day. It wasn't enough that she was unwed and pregnant—and that would be plenty for the gossips to chew on its own—but they were also going to brand her a giant slut because her last breakup had been quite public and fodder for the gossip mill four months ago. All of Dallas knew she was single.

"Nice" girls didn't sleep around and get knocked up. She was supposed to be some sort of role model for the youth of Dallas—a "real lady," as Gwen put it. She was, as Uncle Marcus continuously preached, a Harrison—not some trashy

Hollywood starlet. Promiscuity might fly for the rich and famous somewhere else, but not here. Not in her world. That's why she'd gone to Vegas in the first place.

Society had rules: they weren't fair, and they weren't right, but they were still rules. And she'd just broken a major one.

Oh, God. She'd pulled a lot of stunts, garnered a lot of publicity—both good *and* bad—but nothing like this.

*This* was a nightmare.

Would anyone believe she'd gone the single-mother route intentionally? Used a sperm bank or something? She snorted. Not likely.

The tests with all their positive results seemed to mock her, and she swept them into the trash with one hand. Then she went to the bed to lie down.

In her freshman year of college, she'd invented a boyfriend because she'd seemed like the only girl in her sorority who didn't have one. Leonardo had been Italian, gorgeous and conveniently studying architecture in Rome. Leonardo had served her well that first uncomfortable semester, and she wondered if an imaginary boyfriend would work now. Maybe he'd been tragically killed in a freak scuba-diving accident off the coast of Australia before he even knew she was pregnant….

Right. Even if she could resurrect Leo—and promptly kill him off—there was no way she could claim a long-distance romance. She'd been too visible lately, too often in the society pages to have anyone believe she'd had time to go overseas. In fact, she'd barely left Dallas—aside from one little trip to Las Vegas.

One little trip, that until just a few minutes ago, had held the top spot on her Greatest Memories list. One trip so far outside her reality she hadn't even talked about it to Sabine— beyond the basic details—so she could keep it special and untouched and perfect just as it was in her memory. She didn't bother analyzing or deconstructing it, but she found herself revisiting it a lot, reliving that feeling of freedom...

And Nick.

She thought about Nick much more than could possibly be healthy, remembering his dangerous good looks, the sensation of his body against hers, that devil-take-it attitude that he also brought out in her. Her dreams had become complex and erotic, and she often awoke frustrated and needy, but, even worse, they'd sowed discontent in her waking hours. None of the men in her circle were as good-looking or disarming as Nick, and none of them seemed to understand the real her the way he had—much less bring the real her out from its hiding place behind her family name and social responsibilities.

In short, none of the men here were Nick. And while Nick was totally wrong for her in so many ways, that fact hadn't checked her overactive imagination or made a bit of difference beneath the surface.

Of course, she'd have to tell him at some point. He had a right to know she was carrying his baby. But while she'd fantasized about going back to Vegas in the future and looking him up, *this* hadn't been part of that fantasy. She couldn't even fathom how he might react to the news. Would he be upset? Did he even want children? Or would she be saddling him with a responsibility he didn't want?

Much like Will and Gwen had been saddled with her.

No, this was different. It may have been an accident, but babies were a possible side effect of sex, and if Nick didn't want that responsibility, he shouldn't be...

Jeez, when had she started channeling Uncle Marcus? Evie snorted. Next, she'd be demanding Nick marry her like this was the Dark Ages or something....

The proverbial lightbulb went off. The answer to all her problems was unbelievably simple: she needed a husband.

Everything would be fine if she got married: there'd be no embarrassment to the family, no heart attacks for Uncle Marcus, no explosions from Will, no gossip in the society pages.

Well, there'd be a little of that, considering she was getting married so quickly to someone whom she hadn't been connected with in the past, but she could survive that fallout. The romantic idea of eloping—and that gossip—could be ridden out, and in another month or so she could announce she was pregnant.

This was perfect. Relief spread through her body, and feeling much better, she rolled out of the bed and to her feet. She had the bones of a plan now; she just needed to flesh them out. Energy flowed through her as the plan started to solidify. She'd go to Vegas tomorrow and marry Nick.

*What if Nick doesn't want to get married?* the little voice in her head asked.

That was the hitch in her plan. She didn't know how Nick would respond to the news he was going to be a father, and she really didn't know how he felt about marriage. What would she do if he said no?

Nick wasn't going to say no. He couldn't. He'd want to do the right thing.

And if he didn't? Well, she was a Harrison, and she'd just have to make him an offer he couldn't refuse.

Nick crossed the lobby, his body and mind at odds. Something wasn't right—possibly even very wrong—but he couldn't have stayed away if he'd wanted to. His skin had felt tight and hot since he'd found Evie's message on his phone after his meeting with the soon-to-be-former owners of The Zoo.

Her message was the stuff of teenage male fantasy: "I'm at the Bellagio. I'll be here all day, so call or just come on by when you can." She'd left a phone and room number, and his body had reacted like she'd run a hand over him.

But when Evie left almost four weeks ago, she'd seemed unsure when—or even if—she'd be back in Vegas. To hear from her so quickly…well, it was a stroke to his ego, but also disconcerting. He knew something wasn't right—he could hear it in her voice—but he was headed for her hotel right now because he wasn't thinking with his big head at the moment.

Maybe he was just being paranoid. Looking for problems where none existed. He couldn't shake the feeling, though, even as he knocked on her door.

Evie was a bit slow answering, and while she looked happy to see him, her smile was hesitant—not that dazzling, mega-watt one he remembered so well. "It's good to see you again. Come on in." She held the door open for him, turning her cheek up for a chaste kiss as he passed.

Not exactly the greeting his body had hoped for, and the alarm bells rang louder. The bells were temporarily muted, though, by the realization he wasn't in an ordinary hotel room. Evie was staying in a suite—and a damn nice one at that.

"How've you been?" Evie led him to the sofa and indicated he should sit. Her spine ramrod straight, she perched on the edge of the sofa and clasped her hands in her lap.

"Good. And you?"

Evie's smile faltered, but she recovered quickly. "I'm well, thank you. I'm glad you came." Her voice was strained, teetering on the edge of something.

"And I'm glad you called. I didn't think you'd be able to return to Vegas so soon."

This was awkward. Evie was acting strangely—too polite, too formal and totally unlike the woman he remembered. She was casually dressed in jeans and a green top that brought out the color of her eyes, and her auburn hair was tied back in a long ponytail that draped over her shoulder. But she could have easily been wearing white gloves and a ball dress for all the cool formality of her attitude. If it weren't for the suffocating tension and the pinched look she wore, he almost expected her to offer him tea and a crumpet at any moment.

"Would you like something to drink? A snack, maybe?"

He bit back the absurd laugh and hid it by clearing his throat. "Evie, what's wrong? You're acting…" He searched for the right word. For lack of anything better, he added, "Weird."

Her shoulders sagged a little and she ran a hand across her face. "I know. I've been trying to figure out how to say this, but there's just no good way."

There were those alarm bells again, clanging with intensity as Evie took a deep breath. "Then spit it out."

She blew out the air noisily and met his eyes. Hers were bleak, slightly haunted. "I'm pregnant."

The surprise at her announcement was minimal, but it didn't keep him from feeling as if he'd been punched in the stomach with the confirmation. Where to start…? "You're sure?"

Evie cocked her head. "Very. And, yes, I'm also sure you're the father."

"I wasn't going to ask that." The sick feeling in his stomach and the million other things his brain was trying to process put more bite in those words than he intended.

"Sorry. There was no offense intended, but it is—*would be*—a reasonable question for you to ask, especially since we used protection."

"Fat lot of good that did, huh?" He'd known Evie was going to be trouble; he just hadn't known how much at the time. Now, he was in deep.

Evie shrugged. "Nothing's one hundred percent. However, you should know that I also plan to keep the baby."

He'd come to that conclusion already. She wouldn't spend the money coming here to tell him if she planned to terminate the pregnancy. The first of the knots in his stomach untwisted with that knowledge. Which meant she… "So you need money?"

Her eyebrows went up in surprise. "No. I don't need any money. I'm fully able to support this baby by myself."

A moment too late he realized that was a stupid question to ask. Evie was staying in a suite at the Bellagio; that in itself was proof she didn't need financial support. He'd thought before how Evie looked "expensive," and obviously she was. But just *how* expensive was a question mark. He shouldn't judge her based on his mother's actions, but beautiful rich women…

Evie continued, unaware of his thoughts. "And I'm also happy to work out a visitation agreement that will be agreeable to us both—totally dependent on how much involvement you'd like have to have with the baby, of course."

Involvement? Visitation? Damn it, he'd forgotten for a moment that Evie lived in Dallas. His child was going to be a thousand miles away, and his mind began to race with questions and possibilities and…

"But there *is* something I need from you."

That stopped his thoughts. Evie was about to drop the other shoe. Her eyes were serious, and she looked as if she was steeling herself for what she wanted to say. If she didn't need money, then what? Cautiously, he asked, "And that would be…?"

She took another deep breath. "I need you to marry me."

The words hung in the air as he waited for the punch line. There didn't seem to be one. "Excuse me?"

Evie shot to her feet and began to pace. "I know, it sounds old-fashioned in this day and age, but I need you to marry me."

"You said you didn't need financial support."

"And I don't. *Seriously.* I have more money than I know what to do with." Evie rolled her eyes, making that sound like a bad thing. "What I don't have is a hus-husband," she tripped over the word, "and for me, that's a *huge* problem." Her hands were moving frantically as she spoke, and she finally clasped them together. Maybe he'd read this situation wrong. Evie was certainly agitated; maybe she was worried, scared… "I know this sounds really strange, but I have to get married. I can*not* be an unwed mother."

So much for *that* thought. Or any quaint thoughts about a child needing two parents or even a token compliment thrown his way. This was about her. "Embarrassed, are you, for getting knocked up?"

"It's not embarrassment—at least not for me. I'm going to end up in the papers, yes, but it's my family I'm concerned about."

Her pregnancy was newsworthy? That sick feeling started to settle in his stomach again. There was more to this story, and he wasn't going to like it. "You're not making any sense at all."

"My family is… They're…well…hell." She met his eyes steadily. "We're what you might call 'prominent' in Dallas, if you get my meaning. My brother runs the family's company and my sister-in-law is Gwen Sawyer-Harrison—the one they call 'Miss Behavior'—and she wrote all these etiquette books. We are society- and gossip-column fodder no matter *what* we do, and I'm their current favorite topic at the moment. Don't believe me? Look me up on Google. Evangeline Harrison. If I so much as *sneeze* in public it makes the news. Turning up pregnant… I can't even imagine what they'll say." She shook her head and shuddered. "Actually, I can. And it's going to be ugly."

The implications of her words finally sunk in. Evie was a socialite. An attention-seeking, famous-for-being-rich-and-beautiful socialite. His stomach turned over. Of all the women who came to Las Vegas looking for a good time, *he* managed to find the one who represented everything he most despised.

And she was carrying his baby.

Good Lord. It had to be a Rocco family trait: knock up a

rich-girl-gone-slumming. He had turned into his father. And his kid was going to be severely messed up when Evie decided being a mom didn't mesh well with her high-glam lifestyle. No, he could protect his child from that. He had what his father didn't: money. His child wouldn't grow up in the projects once its mother got over the urge to play Mommy and wanted her old life back—the life that didn't have a child in it.

Evie was staring at him wide-eyed and expectant, but there was worry in that stare. Three weeks ago, he wouldn't have pegged her as a socialite, but then she hadn't been acting like one. And he didn't have reason to look beyond the surface.

Not that women like that had much depth, anyway. The fact she was here, more concerned for herself and her reputation, proved that. "So the Dallas debutante can't face the music at home for her little Vegas-escape weekend."

Her eyes narrowed. "Don't 'poor-little-rich-girl' me. You don't know squat about me or my life at home. If it were just about me, I wouldn't give a flip about what the papers said or what anyone thought. But Will and Gwen will be hurt, disappointed and embarrassed. The consequences of my actions are going to affect more people than just me. My family…" Her voice cracked and she cleared her throat. "I'm just trying to mitigate the damage. To contain the fallout so it doesn't land all over the people I love. The easiest way to do that is to get married. Preferably to you, since you're the father of the child I'm carrying."

Interesting how the baby hadn't figured anywhere into that speech. Had Evie given *any* thought to the child? Or him for that matter? He was supposed to jump to attention, relish the opportunity to marry her exalted self? "And if I'm not amenable to getting married?"

The air seemed to rush out of Evie, and she sagged into a chair. "Then I'll figure something else out. I'm not sure *what* that will be exactly….” She propped her elbows on her knees and rested her chin on her hands. “Are you saying marriage is totally out of the question? Or are you willing to hear my proposal?”

He crossed his arms and leaned back in his seat. Oh, he couldn't *wait* to hear this. “I thought 'I need you to marry me' was your proposal.”

Evie rolled her eyes. “Want me to get down on one knee?” She shrugged. “So it wasn't flowers and romance. Think of it as a business arrangement if it helps. We get married—as soon as possible if that works for you—and you only need to stay married to me for a year or so. Sometime after the baby is born, we can file for a simple, amicable, no-fault divorce.” That word slammed into him, driving home his earlier concerns. “I do need you to come to Dallas and make nice with my family and smile for the papers, but otherwise, I won't interfere with your day-to-day life. I'll be moving here—”

That nicely addressed one problem, but… “Why?”

“It makes sense. Why wouldn't I move to be with my husband? And this is far enough away to keep me out of the spotlight at home.” The corner of her mouth curved down briefly.

“And that's a good thing?” Women like Evie usually thrived on attention—the more the better.

“I've spent enough time in the fishbowl. Some anonymity will do me good.” She cleared her throat again. “But, this is the digital age, so for the sake of appearances, it might be better if we lived together—as roommates only, of course—but if that's out of the question for you, we can figure something else out.”

But which part? The living as roommates or living together at all? She'd put some thought into this. But who on earth got married and then lived as roommates only? *Probably the same kind of person who planned their divorce before they proposed.* "That's it?" he asked sarcastically. "You're not asking much, are you?"

"I *know* it's a lot to ask—and it will cramp your dating style a bit—" her mouth twisted, and he disliked the implication he picked up women in bars as a regular habit "—but all I really ask is that you don't do anything that could get back to my family, or Dallas for that matter, and cause embarrassment for me, my family or the baby." She paused and bit her lip. Something else was coming…. "And you'll need to sign a prenup."

Evie had thrown a lot at him in the last few minutes, and he was still trying to process all of the information. She seemed to take his silence as disagreement, though, and reached for a manila file on the coffee table. "I'll give you a few minutes to read it over, and then…and then we'll talk more." She stood without making eye contact and went to the minibar, where she poured a soda with intentional slowness.

Curious, he flipped open the file. It was a pretty standard agreement: anything Evie had before their marriage—and damn, it *was* substantial—stayed hers. Upon her death, her assets went into a trust managed by her attorney for their child—or children, he noted with surprise. Likewise, everything of his remained his, but without a codicil for the children if something happened to him. She obviously hadn't told whoever drew up this contract she was pregnant already, because there were clauses regarding her inheritance and her heirs if there were no children from the marriage. Darkly, he realized that she'd left him a nice settlement in case of her death.

If he'd been looking to get married, it would be a sweet deal. But he hadn't been looking to get married. The baby—*his* baby—changed everything.

But in case of divorce… "What the hell is this, Evie?"

Nick could tell by the tensing of her shoulders she'd been waiting for him to reach that section.

She faced him with bravado. "That's your settlement. It's rather standard, actually, to set a fixed sum for each year of marriage. In our case…well, I wanted to compensate you for the inconvenience of marrying me."

*Inconvenience* was an interesting word choice. So was *compensate.* "Sounds like a bribe to me."

Her jaw dropped. "It's not a bribe—"

"Then why is the next clause a nondisclosure agreement that forfeits that money if I talk?"

"I'd like some privacy, *some* part of my life I don't have to worry about making the news. That clause isn't anything out of the ordinary, and the money—"

"I don't want your money, Evie."

"But—"

"I believed you when you said you didn't need my money. Trust me when I say I don't *want* yours. I don't need a stud fee. That deed was done for free."

Evie turned a shade of red that clashed with her hair. Then she squared her shoulders and looked at him coolly. "There's no need to be crude. I was only trying to be fair to you."

Politeness dripped off every word. Watching Evie retreat behind a wall of good manners would be amusing in any other situation, but bordered on absurd now. "I don't see anything about custody arrangements."

"Because most people aren't pregnant when they sign pre-nups, and you can't make custody arrangements for children that don't exist yet." Evie was still unfailingly polite, but he could hear the undercurrent of frustration in her voice. "Those arrangements come with divorce papers."

Custody arrangements were foremost in his mind at the moment. Damn it. He had a master plan and marriage—to anyone—hadn't been in it. He was ahead of his schedule, but marrying a spoiled socialite wasn't on that schedule *anywhere.* And a baby…

Risk of fallout or not, he didn't doubt Evie would go home to have this child if he refused to marry her. He didn't give a damn about her reputation or the "problems" that would cause her family, but it did create problems for him. One, he wouldn't be able to keep an eye on Evie while she was pregnant. She could do God-knows-what for the next nine months and cause the baby to have all kinds of problems.

He was a hands-on project manager: marrying Evie would give him oversight of this pregnancy.

Secondly, refusing to marry Evie now could put him in legal difficulties later when he *did* sue for custody. She could use this moment against him later, claiming she'd offered him the chance to claim paternity and he'd refused.

The fact she had money—and a powerful family—added a degree of difficulty to the situation. If on the off-chance she did decide to fight him in the future, she'd have the where-withal; he didn't need to give her any additional ammunition.

That was a slim chance anyway. Her family probably wouldn't want a reminder of Evie's mistake. They wouldn't want his less-than-blue-blood or his blue-collar DNA sullying the Harrison bloodline.

But marrying Evie would give him all kinds of rights and give him some control over the situation. If Evie proved to be a good mother, he didn't *have* to divorce her, and his child could grow up with two parents. People married for less noble causes and managed to live somewhat harmoniously. She'd called it a business arrangement. Crude wording, but true.

Decision made, he took a pen out of his pocket and drew a line through the divorce settlement clause and initialed the change. "You'll need to initial that before you sign. We can get it witnessed and notarized when we get our marriage license."

He didn't realize how tense Evie was until he saw her close her eyes as the relief washed over her. When she opened them, the relief there was tempered by an uncertain discomfort and cautious disbelief.

Nick knew exactly how she felt.

Dear Lord, was she actually going to *do* this? Evie felt a weight lift off her shoulders only to be replaced by a strange sick feeling in her stomach. She'd spent all her time working on the plan to get Nick to agree, but she hadn't thought beyond that. Marrying Nick sounded so good in theory—the baby would know its father, she wouldn't have to face the press—but now that it was about to become *reality,* she was afraid she was about to make a huge mistake.

For both her and the baby. This baby wouldn't lack for anything, and she worried now that bringing Nick into the situation instead of just facing the music alone might not be the best idea in the long run.

Because this Nick wasn't the one she remembered. The fun-loving, laid-back Nick of a few weeks ago had been replaced by a man with a hard jaw who very early on in this "meeting" had began to look at her with what she could only describe as distaste. And she didn't understand why.

After all, she'd worked very hard to make her proposal as palatable for him as possible. She'd rehearsed this; she wasn't coming to him all needy or trying to play on his conscience. She was offering him a very fair arrangement, and he was acting like…like…

His sarcasm, the cold bite in his words, the way he was scowling at her… *Ugh.* Topped with the cool efficiency as he flipped through the prenup and discussed details… She almost backed out of the whole plan because she'd be better off dealing with Will than Nick. At least she knew how to handle Will when he got like this.

For someone whose plan was coming together, who was getting exactly what she wanted, she felt as if she was

strapped in a guillotine, unsure whether she dreaded or welcomed the fall of the blade. She gave Nick one more chance
to back down. "Are we really going to do this? Like right
*now?*"

One dark brow arched at her. "Why wait? This was your
idea, not mine. Cold feet already?"

*Yes.* "No, not at all." *Now what?* Lighten the mood, that's
what. "So…what do we do? Go to the courthouse? Elvis at
a drive-through?"

Nick thought for a moment, and Evie would have given her
trust fund to know exactly what was going through his mind.
"I actually have a few things to do first. Give me a couple of
hours and then we'll go."

A couple of hours. She felt the guillotine blade slide a little
bit. That short of a reprieve wouldn't give her much time to
get her head sorted back out. "Okay." What was she going to
do with herself for a couple of hours? *Besides* hyperventilate.

"Do you have a dress?"

That snapped her back to the conversation. "Pardon me?"

"A dress? To get married in? I'm assuming you'll want pictures to show your family, and you won't want to be in jeans."

She hadn't thought of that. She mentally sorted through her
suitcase and came up empty. That showed how out of it she
was; she came to Vegas to get married and didn't even pack
a nice dress. Maybe deep down, she'd been expecting—
hoping?—this plan would fall through and not happen at all.
"You know, I don't. I guess I can shop for something while
you…you do…whatever it is you need to go do."

Nick nodded, but his scowl didn't diminish at all. "I'll
pick you up at eight, then."

She walked Nick to the door, the uncomfortable tension
between them so different than what she remembered from
before. When the door closed behind him, Evie leaned against
it and banged her head gently. This was absurd; she was mar-

KIMBERLY LANG 63

rying a man she barely knew simply because she was carrying his child. How had she ended up here?

She'd allowed herself one tiny romanticized daydream where this conversation worked out completely differently.... But no. This was a business agreement. She knew that. She swallowed her disappointment Nick was treating it as such.

Evie looked at her watch and sighed. She needed a dress, but the last thing she felt like doing was shopping. Thankfully, there were plenty of great shops right here in the Bellagio. They'd have something for her to wear.

By fifteen to eight, she'd showered and redone her hair and makeup and was sliding the zipper up on the simple ivory sheath she'd found. It was perfect for a simple wedding, and were the circumstances different, she'd be thrilled to wear it. This was a far cry from the princess-style wedding she and Gwen had talked about when she was a teenager. Not that that kind of wedding had been her dream—she always imagined something more intimate and private—but this wedding was falling far short of *any* kind of romantic fantasy.

Instead, she was getting ready for her wedding alone in a hotel suite. She should have let Bennie come with her; it just seemed wrong to get married without any of her family and friends around.

Her fiancé was gorgeous and sexy and made her heart pound to think about him; Nick was practically the groom of adolescent fantasy weddings in the flesh. But...

This wasn't going to be a romantic story she'd share with her child in the years to come, that was for sure. The disappointment in her stomach was real—a physical pain. She'd always assumed that when she did get married, it would be forever; a marriage like Will and Gwen's, like her parents'.

The sharp knock at her door startled her. A glance at the clock told her Nick was punctual, if nothing else.

She said goodbye to her girlish fantasy and faced reality.

Evie slid her feet into her shoes and grabbed her purse. With one last deep breath to steady her nerves and fortify her resolve, she went to get married.

# CHAPTER FIVE

WHEN EVIE OPENED THE DOOR, she was steeled for the worst.
She wasn't prepared, though, for the physical reaction that
slammed into her, stealing her breath and causing heat to coil
through her veins. She'd seen Nick in jeans; she'd seen him
in a work-appropriate shirt and tie earlier, but in black slacks
and a black button-down silk shirt...*damn*. He looked wicked
and delicious, and only showing up naked at her door could
have affected her pulse more.

He had showered and shaved, and his dark hair fell
casually over his forehead in a tousle most men would have
to spend hours to achieve. If things were just a little different...

But the arching of Nick's eyebrow was a harsh reminder
of the reality of the situation. Things weren't different. Things
were what they were. He tempered that reminder, though,
with a simple, "You look nice, Evie," that caused her heart to
stutter regardless.

"Thank you. You look pretty good yourself." She pulled
the door closed behind her and gripped her handbag tightly
to keep her fingers from sliding over that silk shirt to feel the
man beneath. As they walked toward the elevator, Nick's
hand landed on the small of her back.

It was a simple gesture—commonplace, even—but Evie

felt as if she'd been touched by a live wire. Had she really offered Nick a marriage in name only? That they'd live simply as roommates? She had to be insane. How had she forgotten the magnetism of this man?

In the close confines of the elevator, each breath she took was filled with his scent, and her thighs were trembling as they descended.

"That's a nice dress. Didn't they have anything in white?"

She cut her eyes at him. Was that an insult or a tease? His dry tone didn't help; he could have been discussing the interior decor of the elevator. "White's not a good color for me. Too harsh against my skin tone."

Nick merely nodded, which didn't tell her anything,

She swallowed. "So, what's the plan?"

"Kevin and Lottie are meeting us in the lobby. We'll go to the license bureau first—"

*Whoa.* "I'm sorry, who are Kevin and Lottie?"

"Kevin is my friend and business partner. Lottie is his wife. I couldn't get married without telling them."

*That* caused her conscience to twinge in guilt, and she thought sadly of her family again. "I see."

The elevator doors opened, and Nick took her hand as she stepped out, stopping her just beyond the threshold. "My friends don't know the true circumstances surrounding this wedding, and I'd like to keep it that way—although for different reasons than you."

She hadn't thought about what Nick might tell his friends and family. Realizing all the things she'd forgotten in her plan was quickly becoming a full-time job. "Of course. One happy couple, coming up."

Nick smiled for the first time and butterflies battered her insides. He didn't let go of her hand, either, and a nice warmth moved through her as they crossed the lobby in the direction of a couple wearing bright smiles.

"Kevin, Lottie, this is Evie."

Kevin had average Irish good looks—tall and ruddy—an open, honest face and a contagious grin that put her at ease almost immediately. Lottie, in contrast, was petite, with beautiful olive skin and long black hair that hung to her waist. Lottie immediately wrapped Evie in a hug that made her feel welcome and slightly guilty for deceiving this nice woman.

"You're even more beautiful than Nick said," Lottie gushed, "but I'm sure we're going to be great friends, regardless."

Evie was still reeling over the news Nick had told these people she was beautiful as Lottie rushed on. "Later, you'll have to tell me how you managed to snare Nick. I'd all but given up on him finding someone."

"Let her breathe, Lottie," Kevin admonished his wife. Turning his grin at Evie, he extended a hand and continued, "You're a brave girl, tying yourself to this guy."

Evie felt a bit overwhelmed and unsure of what to say. "I'm very happy to meet you both. Nick has told me so much about you."

From the identical shocked expressions on Kevin and Lottie's faces, she worried she'd stepped in something, but she wasn't sure what. She knew she wasn't the *best* actress, but had she blown it already?

Then Kevin laughed. "Nick talking. That's a first."

Confused, she looked at Nick, who merely shrugged. *Great. That's helpful.*

Lottie took her husband's hand. "I told you she'd have to be something special."

She didn't feel very special at the moment. "He is the strong, silent type, isn't he? That's okay, because I can talk enough for both of us."

Lottie beamed, and Evie wanted to like her—felt as if she *could* really like her and maybe have a friend in Las Vegas already—but the guilt was killing her. If the guilt of deception was this bad just with Nick's friends, how on earth would she survive her family?

Nick continued to hold her hand as they followed Kevin and Lottie out and into a waiting SUV. Kevin held the door open for her with a mock bow. "I'll be your driver for the evening. Sit back and relax. First stop, marriage license bureau."

She'd been surprised to learn that any government agency in the world was open until midnight seven days a week, but as she filled out the paperwork for her marriage license along with several other couples, she understood the necessity of it in Las Vegas.

Her license was still hot off the printer when Kevin herded them back into the car and screeched out of the parking lot. Just a few minutes later, she was entering a chapel, and Lottie was pushing a small bouquet of roses and daisies into her hands.

Her chest constricted, and it became difficult to breathe. *Back out. Run. Forget this whole plan.* Then Nick tucked her arm under his. She jumped in surprise.

He leaned close to her ear and whispered, "You're not planning on ditching me at the altar, are you?"

The humor in his voice banked the onset of her panic attack, and she looked up to see an amused glint in his eyes. "Actually, I am."

"Too late," he countered, as a balding man waved them forward and Kevin and Lottie took their places on either side of them.

She'd never realized how quick a wedding ceremony actually was, and the minister was looking to her for a response before she'd had a chance to catch her breath. Nick's "I do" seemed to boom in her head, even though she knew he'd said it at normal volume.

At least she wasn't in a tacky chapel being married by an Elvis with fake sideburns. This chapel was actually rather nice: understated and charming, lit by soft candlelight and peaceful. While she'd been floundering in confusion and trying to find a decent dress to wear, Nick had been busy planning something nice for their wedding. Her stomach gave a funny flip at the idea.

She panicked when the minister asked for the rings, but Lottie touched her arm gently and passed her a heavy gold band with a faint outline of Celtic knots across the surface. Evie fought back tears as Nick took her hand and slid a matching band over her knuckle. This wedding was perfect and beautiful and totally false. It was killing her.

When she turned her head, she saw Nick's strong profile as he listened to the minister pronounce them husband and wife. Nick turned to her and smiled wryly as he lowered his head to brush a gentle kiss across her lips. Time seemed to stop, and her heart beat faster as that kiss arced through her, stirring her blood with desire. But the gentleness of it caused her stomach to flip over again, making the moment feel poignant and important and one she wanted to remember for the rest of her life. She leaned in, pressing her mouth more fully against his, and she felt his lips soften as if he were going to deepen the kiss, make it…

Then Kevin clapped and Lottie was snapping pictures and horrid reality crashed in. Rice landed on her shoulders and slid inside her dress, and they were back outside with a certificate proving they were married before she could wrap her head around it. Another couple was already taking their place at the chapel doors; a very young couple with ear-to-ear grins and an inability to keep their hands off each other. She was suddenly irrationally jealous.

Needing a moment to regain her equilibrium, Evie pretended great interest in the envelope containing her marriage certificate. The date and "Mr. and Mrs. Nicolas Rocco" were written in fancy script across the front.

*Mr. and Mrs.* She was now Evie Rocco—a name she hadn't known until a couple of hours ago. Or maybe she should do like Gwen and hyphenate: Evangeline Harrison-Rocco. No. Too many letters. She guessed it didn't matter too much; she wasn't going to be keeping the name for very long.

That bothered her more than she liked.

Nick was being very quiet; something she found a little odd, but Kevin and Lottie didn't seem at all bothered. Evie got the feeling Nick's silence really was normal as far as they were concerned. In the backseat of Kevin's SUV, she leaned as close to Nick as her seat belt would allow.

"Thank you for arranging something so nice. I really didn't want to get married at a drive-through," she whispered, hoping Kevin and Lottie would think they were simply nuzzling newlyweds.

He shrugged. "Thank Lottie. It was mostly her doing."

*Oh.* So much for warm fuzzies. "I see," she whispered, trying to keep the deflation out of her voice by thinking of the way that kiss at the chapel had almost…

"None of that," Kevin shouted from the driver's seat, and Evie jumped back to her side of the backseat. "I know you're eager to get to your bridal suite and—" Lottie's hand smacking his arm cut Kevin off.

Evie choked back a laugh. Lottie and Kevin reminded her a little of Will and Gwen, the way she kept pulling him back into line. The amusement faded, though, at the thought of how disappointed Will and Gwen were going to be when she showed up at home with her new husband.

"*Ahem,*" Kevin started again. "Lottie has a surprise for you two first."

She felt she'd had enough surprises recently, but it would be ungracious to say so. But déjà vu set in along with surprise when Kevin parked in the lot at Blue and indicated they should get out.

"Obviously your last date here worked out pretty well," he grinned lasciviously and winked, "so Lottie thought it might be a nice place to start off your new life together."

Nick's eyebrows drew together. "The roof is booked tonight."

"It *was*," Kevin corrected. He looked at Evie. "I had to tick off a few B-list celebs by cancelling their party, but they were happy enough to be rebooked in the VIP room at Starlight."

"Kevin," Nick growled.

Kevin waved him off and leaned into Evie as they walked. "Nick's partial to Blue since it's his pride and joy, but really, Starlight will work for them just fine. It's not like he's really losing any money off of it."

All kinds of details were pressing their way through the fog that had entered her brain the moment she met Nick, and now she needed some answers. Answers she *should* have gotten before she waded into this, but Nick and clearheaded thinking didn't come as a package deal. Evie plastered a smile on her face. "Could you excuse us for just a second? I haven't had a chance to be alone with Nick since…"

Kevin lifted his hands as he backed away. "No problem. Lottie and I will go check on your surprise. Just don't get too carried away." He winked and disappeared through Blue's door.

Evie grabbed Nick's hand and pulled him out of the direct line of sight of the door. "Explain to me how you 'know the owner' of this nightclub?"

Nick cleared his throat. "Well…"

"You and Kevin own this place, don't you? This is how you're business partners, isn't it?" Why hadn't he told her?

"Not exactly."

"Oh." She felt foolish and wished it was a little darker in this parking lot so he couldn't see the flush she felt on her cheeks.

"I own Blue. Kevin runs a different part of the business."

She felt her jaw drop. "You own Blue outright?"

He smirked. "And four other clubs."

How'd she miss *that* piece of information? All those details she'd overlooked—first in lust, and then in her marriage panic—jumped to the forefront to scream at her. Nick's expensive car, the obviously custom cut of his clothes, the deference of the employees here at Blue and Starlight...

"Including Starlight?" She waved the question away before Nick could reply; she didn't really need an answer that obvious. "No wonder you didn't need a divorce settlement spelled out in the prenup."

Nick stiffened. "So you did think you could buy me off with money. Go slumming and use your trust fund to get out of the mess?"

She lifted her chin at the insult. "I'm not even going to dignify that with a response."

"Don't bother to try." His jaw hardened. "You're not the only one who can afford to support this child."

*That seemed a gross understatement.* "I see that now. Why didn't you just tell me this that first night?"

The corner of his mouth curled again, but this time it was in sarcasm. "Probably for the same reason you didn't mention your trust fund."

She would *not* feel guilty, damn it, for not advertising who she was on their first date. "I wanted you to think I was just an average girl." Her voice dropped. "I guess we both surprised each other."

Nick crossed his arms over his chest. "And this disappoints you somehow?"

His attitude rankled her. The last warm fuzzy feeling from earlier evaporated. "Not at all. In fact, it will make things much easier at home. Less speculation about *why* we got married."

He looked at her stomach pointedly. "I think the *why* will become obvious soon enough."

She wanted to hit him just hard enough to knock that sarcastic look off his face. "Yes, but at least no one should be able to accuse *you* of knocking me up just to get a piece of my inheritance."

"Or think you're a fool for letting it happen," he finished for her, the words dripping with bitter disdain.

The urge to smack him was growing stronger by the second. "Exactly. It's all about me, you know."

"Isn't it?" he challenged.

Anger battled insult and came out as outrage. "*Excuse* me? What do you mean by *that?*"

"Couldn't you have just as easily claimed to have fallen hard for your personal trainer and avoided all this? I'm sure he would love the 'settlement' you outlined *and* served your purpose nicely enough."

She opened her mouth to inform him she didn't *have* a personal trainer before she realized the stupidity of that argument. "If you have some kind of problem with me—" Nick snorted and she dug her nails into her palms. "Which obviously you *do,* why on earth did you agree to marry me?"

"As you said, it's *my* baby." Nick's possessive tone grated across her already raw nerves.

"You seem to be taking that at face value. No doubts about paternity? No real fears about my trainer?"

He stiffened. "Like you'd come all the way to Vegas to get me to marry you if the baby wasn't mine. It's too easily disproved."

"Are you two coming or not?" Lottie's head appeared around the door as she shouted for them.

"In a second," Nick called, and Lottie disappeared back inside. "Come on," he muttered at her.

She took a step back. She'd been insulted enough for one day. "No way. I'm going back to my hotel now."

A muscle twitched in his jaw. "This was your idea, Evie."

"It was *your* idea to involve your friends. Not mine."

Nick's eyes narrowed. "If you can't pull this off in front of Kevin and Lottie—who, by the way, are genuinely happy for us—then you don't have a prayer of convincing *your* family."

Dear God, he was right. She needed to screw her head on straight, suck it up and ride out this rodeo. She took a deep breath, trying to calm herself. She was doing what was best for the baby, for her family—for everyone. She needed to stay focused on that. The deed was done—she was pregnant and safely married—now she had to follow through.

If she managed to survive this with her sanity and dignity intact, she would never, *ever,* step outside the lines again. *I swear, God, really.* She'd live the most boring, circumspect, politically correct life Dallas had ever seen.

*If* she managed to survive.

She nodded her agreement at Nick and plastered a smile on her face as he took her elbow and led her to the door. To her surprise and chagrin, her skin tingled where it touched his, and getting back in close proximity caused an uptick in her pulse.

That *if* was getting more questionable by the moment.

Kevin might have initially been skeptical about this sudden wedding, but Lottie—who just happened to be right there when Nick called—had let her inner romantic out to run free at his first mention of the word *married.* Even Kevin had warmed to the idea rather quickly—thanks to Lottie—trapping Nick in their romanticized reading of the situation before he could tell Kevin the truth. He hadn't planned on misleading Kevin about this wedding, but he got in too deep too fast to extricate himself gracefully.

As the elevator doors opened to the roof, he realized he should have stopped them both long before now. The Sheik's Tent was romantically lit with candles, and Lottie had sent someone up here with flowers and a miniature wedding cake. Kevin popped the cork on a bottle of champagne as the elevator doors closed behind them.

Lottie was beaming, but apologetic. "It's not much, but on such short notice…"

He looked at Evie, whose shoulders seemed to square as Lottie spoke, and noticed the kind smile on her face. "It's beautiful, Lottie. So much more than I could've hoped for. Thank you."

Evie could pull out the grace and graciousness in a millisecond. In fact, he was beginning to notice how the more uncomfortable she got in a situation, the more polite and amiable she became. Except with him. Evie was shooting daggers in his direction every time she caught his eye, but she played her part well, holding his hand, trailing her fingers down his arm playfully and generally driving him insane with her touch. But with Lottie and Kevin, she turned on the charm, accepting their toast with the tiniest of sips of the excellent champagne, admiring the cake and expressing what looked like genuine interest in them both.

All the hallmarks of the society belle she was. He needed to remember that, and not get blinded by her beauty or her charm. Nick could easily picture Evie at her debutante ball, a charity gala, even a polo match, working the crowd with charm and ease. But Kevin and Lottie left as soon as they cut the cake—Kevin making ribald comments about needing privacy while Lottie hushed him and dug elbows into his ribs.

Their exit left him alone with his wife, who shut off that charm the moment the elevator doors closed behind their wedding guests.

Evie lapsed into silence, setting aside her champagne glass and foraging behind the bar for a bottle of water. She sank onto the low sofa, only to jump to her feet again as if it burned her. The flush rising over the V of her neckline made clear the memories of that sofa were fresh in her mind, as well.

Although his earlier compliment had been rather offhand, something that seemed appropriate to say in the silence, Evie looked more than just nice. She looked beautiful, as stunning as the first time he laid eyes on her, but tonight her elegance and good breeding were on display, as well as her charms. Her skin glowed in the candlelight, and the simple dress hugged the delicious curves he remembered with stark, haunting clarity.

And while he was touched by Lottie's thoughtfulness, he rather wished they'd not brought him and Evie here, of all places. Returning to the scene of one of his most erotic memories with the woman who played the starring role had his body hard and aching, but tonight was a far cry from last time. Instead of the sensual, exciting Evie of his memory, this Evie was distant, wary and bordering on hostile.

She was also his pregnant wife, and the stunning absurdity of *that* knowledge was enough to send him behind the bar to search for something stronger than champagne.

"So we seem to be stuck here. What do we do now?" Evie asked, as the silence stretched out between them.

He raised an eyebrow at her, and she blushed deeper.

"I mean, the official part is taken care of, so where do we go from here?" She twisted the gold band on her ring finger as she spoke.

His body had a grand idea, and it circled around Evie wearing nothing but that gold band. Somehow, he knew Evie wouldn't be amenable to *that*. "Are you hungry?" he asked lamely for lack of something better. Lottie's minions had left a simple cold dinner behind the bar.

"No. My stomach's all tied up in knots at the moment. Food is the last thing I need. But I guess we *do* need to stay here for a little while, at least. You go ahead, if you're hungry."

Evie pulled out a chair and sat at the small table, the politeness back in her voice and her hands folded neatly on the table. "We can make a few plans, get our story straight."

"What's there to get straight?"

Her tone all business, she jumped into the conversation. "I'd really like to avoid dropping two bombs on my family at once. Our elopement will be enough of a shock for them without mentioning the baby. I can call home with *that* news in a couple of weeks—after they've had a chance to recover."

"Unless your family is stupid, surely they'll make the leap from elopement to pregnant."

Evie shrugged. "Maybe not. This isn't the first time I've done something crazy and unexpected." A bitter laugh escaped.

So she did have a wild streak. "This is merely par for the course?"

"I wouldn't say that. Eloping is definitely an extreme even *I* hadn't considered. There will be speculation, of course, about me being pregnant, but I'll be safely up here before any of that gets spinning." She drummed her nails on the glass tabletop, but when he came to take the chair opposite hers, she slid back and moved her hands in her lap. "Since we're mar-married," she stumbled over the word, "I'd like to break the news to my family as soon as possible, and I think it would be more believable if you were with me. Is your schedule flexible enough for you to come to Dallas for a couple of days?"

It wasn't. Especially not with a sale pending on The Zoo. But something in Evie's wide green eyes stopped him from saying so. "I'll need to make a few calls in the morning to arrange things, but we could go to Dallas tomorrow afternoon."

Evie's shoulders dropped in relief, and she nodded. "You could be back here by the weekend, but it may take me a couple more days to get my things together, tie up a few loose ends at work—"

"You have a job?" He couldn't keep the shock out of his voice. Between the state of her finances and the fact she was in Vegas on a Tuesday, he'd assumed being beautiful *was* her primary job.

Her eyes narrowed at him again. "Of course I have a job. It's not much of one, but it's a job."

Most people would describe a job flipping burgers like that, but there was no way Evie worked for minimum wage. But what did someone like Evie do? Honestly curious, he asked her.

"I work in HarCorp's marketing department."

He'd used Google to look up Evie shortly after leaving her hotel this afternoon. In addition to seeing her smiling face at every society event in Dallas worthy of making the paper, he'd found Evie's description of her "family's company" to be misleading. HarCorp was a huge international company with fingers in many different pies. And she worked in their marketing department? The surprise must have shown on his face, and Evie's mouth twisted.

"I've been regulated to PR mostly—doing all the 'public stuff' like charity work and fundraisers—and it's only part-time, but it was the best I could do considering my brother's extreme surprise I'd even want to work for the company." That hollow, bitter laugh escaped again. "I see you're surprised, as well. I realize you can only judge me based on our current fiasco, but I'm not a complete ditz. I graduated at the top of my class and everything."

Oh, he had no doubt of her intelligence, even if everything *else* about her—including how she used that intelligence—was in question. "From finishing school? Let me guess... France?"

Evie bit her lip and he saw her knuckles whiten. Then she lifted her chin and smiled broadly. "Switzerland, actually. But I was really referring to Trinity University's Business

School. I should be able to get a job up here doing something, don't you agree?"

"Why would you want to?" She didn't need to work—even temporarily while she was pregnant. Did she not want to stay home with the baby?

Genuine confusion twisted her face. "What else would I do for the next nine months? Sit around and knit booties? You don't expect me to become president of the Junior League or join the UDC, do you?"

What was she talking about? "I have no idea what either of those are."

This time Evie's laugh was real, and it echoed off the stone walls of the roof. Even though he didn't understand the humor, her laugh reminded him of the Evie he'd met before. "Really? Oh, that's fabulous. I think I'm going to love living in Vegas."

"It's nothing like Dallas," he reminded her.

"And that's one of the many, *many* reasons I love Las Vegas." She eyed him carefully. "You're not press fodder, are you?"

"I don't know what you mean."

"Do you make the papers a lot? Gossip columns, fashion pages, society blogs, anything like that?"

Evie had a skewed view of the world. "Do you honestly think nightclub owners are interesting to the press? In *this* town?"

"I just wanted to be sure." She looked out at the skyline and sighed. When she didn't elaborate, he let the silence spin out until Evie started to shift uncomfortably in her seat and she cleared her throat. "Have we killed enough time up here? Can we go back to the hotel now?"

The absurd reality of the situation—which he'd managed to forget momentarily—settled around him. This was his wedding night, and he was sitting on the roof of Blue with his bride, debating what to do next.

That spark, that sizzling need that marked their first meeting, had been slightly damped by Evie's revelations and the circus of their wedding, but it was still there. The tightening of his body at the thought of what he *should* be doing with Evie on their wedding night was real enough, as had the light in Evie's eyes she hadn't been able to fully hide behind the variety of emotions she'd spiraled through this evening.

She'd blushed when she said she wanted to go back to the hotel, but she'd wanted a marriage in name only, like some sort of a bad movie plot, so he assumed Evie wouldn't be open to his idea of how to kill some time—here *or* at her hotel.

Her next words confirmed that.

"I've had a long day, and I want to go to bed. To sleep," she corrected. "I'm, um, tired. Really tired."

Well, he had his answer. Although every part of him protested, he wasn't going to push as if he was some sort of desperate teenager trying to get into her pants.

This marriage thing had to have some perks attached to it—beyond custody of his child. He'd let Evie think whatever she liked until they got back from Dallas, and then he'd explain the situation to her.

# CHAPTER SIX

COWARD. EVIE PUNCHED her pillow into shape and curled around it as her stomach churned at the thought. She may have become more cautious, better behaved, over the years—with varying degrees of success, granted—but never had she been such an outright, chicken-livered, all-hat-and-no-cattle *coward.*

So now she was alone in her hotel suite on her wedding night, unable to sleep because she couldn't quit berating herself for her cowardice and unable to shake the feeling that, regardless of the circumstances surrounding their wedding, she should be having mind-blowing sex with her new husband right now.

Her blood heated with the memory, the fantasy of what could've been on the agenda for tonight, if she hadn't been such a weenie when Nick turned her question around on her. Despite everything else going on, she'd felt the tension in him, seen the barely banked desire in his eyes. He might not like her very much, but he *did* want her.

And while her body had been all in favor of taking what she could get, her pride was still smarting from his revelations and his treatment of her, and she'd backed down.

If she wasn't such a coward, she'd have asked him straight out *what* his new problem was, but how could you ask someone "Why don't you like me?" without it sounding like a pathetic whine? Was he angry she was pregnant? Did he blame her? Think she did it on purpose? Or had he only been out for a good time and now resented the result? Had she been suckered in by a player and fallen for his lines? That was an unpleasant thought.

The deed was done now. She was married to Nick—at least for the near future.

They'd killed a little more time on the roof—Nick booking plane tickets back to Dallas while she sent Gwen a text inviting herself and a friend over for drinks the next night— before they snuck out the back door of Blue like thieves. Nick had delivered her back here without much conversation, then left. She assumed he went home—wherever that was.

God, she didn't even know where he *lived.*

She couldn't help but wonder if she'd made a grave mistake in her rush to try to fix this situation before it exploded in her face. Nick, at least, seemed game to hold up his end of the bargain—even though he had no real reason to do so— so she should be thankful for that.

Still, it seemed wrong to be married and not have any of the benefits that went with it. *Why* had she opened her big mouth? Hadn't she learned anything about negotiating a contract from listening to Will over the years? Obviously not, or else she wouldn't be burning with frustration right now.

With a groan, she rolled to her other side and looked at the clock. Maybe she'd feel better once she got the showdown at home over with. After she dealt with her family, she could concentrate on sorting out the mess she'd already made of her marriage.

Nick had never been taken home to meet the family before. He wasn't the type of guy women took home to their parents—not since he picked up his prom date had he been expected to make nice with the family. This would be awkward no matter what the circumstances were, but the tension radiating off of Evie had his own nerves on alert in response.

Their conversation—if that's what it could be called—on the flight to Dallas had been stilted at best and circled around their "story." Evie seemed lost in thought most of the time, staring out the window and often dropping off to monosyllabic replies to his questions.

The flight had been delayed, and they'd barely dropped their bags at Evie's place before she was ushering him out the door and muttering about not being late as if tardiness was a capital crime.

He let Evie drive without comment since she knew the way, but her knuckles were white from her grip on the steering wheel. She seemed to be carrying on an interesting conversation with herself, and he couldn't get a word in edgewise. But that graciousness he'd seen her pull out before came into play when they pulled to a stop in front of a high-rise building, and she turned that dazzling smile on the doorman as she handed over her car keys.

In the elevator, she finally looked at him directly, and he saw a spark of energy there he recognized. Evie was steeling herself for a fight, and she was ready for it, even. "Just let me take the lead on this, okay? This won't take long. Just stick to our story like the gospel, and the ugliness will be over quickly."

*Ugliness?*

He saw her set her jaw and take a deep breath as she slid her key into the door, and he wondered *what* the hell kind of family Evie came from. He rather felt as if the guard escorting the princess into the dragon's lair for the sacrifice.

"I'm here!" Evie singsonged as she pushed open the door, and the turnaround in her attitude floored him. She was all smiles and sounded completely carefree. "Anyone home?"

"Evie!" Two boys, maybe six or seven years old, came

thundering down the hallway and launched themselves into Evie's outstretched arms.

"Hey, monsters! Whoa, someone's feeding you too much. You keep growing." She dropped her voice to a whisper. "I thought we had a deal about that."

She gave each of them a big kiss, showing a facet of her personality he hadn't seen yet. Evie liked children—or at least *these* children—and they loved her. That knowledge alleviated a tiny bit of his primary concern.

The boys giggled as they wiped the kisses off, then turned curious green eyes exactly like Evie's on him.

"Nick, these two monsters are Justin and Patrick, my nephews," Evie offered. "This is my friend Nick."

Both boys nodded and extended small, slightly sticky hands for him to shake. "Nice to meet you," they chorused carefully before taking back off down the hallway with shouts of "Mom! Dad! Evie's here!"

"Well, that still needs a little work." Evie laughed. "Don't run," she called after them, and Nick could hear a woman saying the exact same thing as she dodged the children on her way through a doorway to their right.

He'd been expecting a veritable dragon, not a petite woman half a head shorter than Evie with soft, gentle features. She wrapped Evie in a tight hug. "Evie, honey, it's good to see you." She then turned to Nick expectantly.

Evie reached for his arm, her fingers tightening around his bicep. "Nick, this is my sister-in-law, Gwen. Gwen, this is Nick. Nick Rocco."

The possessive touch and the deliberate lack of even a brief explanation of who he was weren't lost on Gwen. She raised an eyebrow at Evie briefly, a smile tugging at her mouth, before she extended a hand to him. "It's lovely to meet you, Nick. Welcome."

"Thank you. And it's nice to meet you, too."

Evie's hand loosened a bit, and her shoulders slipped just a little. What had she expected from him? Did she think he was so low-class he couldn't handle meeting her family without causing embarrassment? His manners might not be as polished as Evie's, but he did have them.

Gwen waved them out of the hall and toward a large room with a great view of Dallas. "Will is on the phone in his office, but he should be out any second now. We can have a drink while we wait."

Hard on her words, a man he assumed had to be Will joined them. Evie's brother didn't seem to be a fire-breathing dragon, either, as he kissed Evie on the cheek and she repeated the introductions. Nick knew he was being assessed as Will shook his hand and cut his eyes at Evie. The man was not subtle at all.

But Evie's family seemed remarkably normal—not at all worth the stress he'd seen from her or the tension she was holding in check behind her smile. The older couple—he really couldn't call them "old" since they only looked to be in their forties—knew something was up. It was clear that they were waiting for Evie to make some kind of announcement, but they were still friendly enough.

He settled back onto a leather sofa and accepted the wine Gwen offered. Evie sat her glass on the table as Will took a chair opposite them and Gwen perched easily—if oddly, considering there wasn't a lack of seating available—on the arm with her husband's hand on her waist.

Gwen leaned forward, her face kind but curious. "Nick Rocco. I don't think I've heard the name before. Would we know your family?"

Evie jumped in before he could answer, her voice bright as she took his hand and twined her fingers through his. "No, Gwen, you wouldn't. Nick's from Las Vegas."

And the air in the room changed at that moment. Evie's statement had been simple and delivered with friendliness, but a gauntlet had been thrown down. Will's eyebrows drew together in a frown, and Gwen's eyes darted toward Evie's hands. Gwen was quick on the uptake. Surprise registered on her face before she lifted her glass and drank deeply.

Will, however, was busy glowering at his sister and hadn't made the same leap his wife had. "Surely I didn't hear that correctly. You met him in Las Vegas, Evie?"

Evie's spine straightened an inch. "Yes, I did."

"When, exactly?" Even Nick could hear the dangerous growl under those words. Evie hadn't been kidding when she said her brother was unhappy about her taking off for a weekend in Sin City.

"Four weeks ago." She took a deep breath. "And I wasn't at work yesterday or today because I went back to Vegas. To get married." She held her hand up to show the gold band on her finger.

"What the—" Will started to roar, only to have Gwen's elbow fly sharply into his ribs. Now Nick understood Gwen's choice of seating. And a little of Evie's stress.

"That's quite a surprise, Evie." Gwen came to hug Evie again, and this time, she hugged him, as well. "Congratulations to you both. I wish you'd given us a little warning, honey. We would've liked to have been there."

While Gwen was all smiles and hugs, Will was shooting dark daggers at him and no doubt planning how to dispose of his dead body. "Did you know she was an heiress?" he snapped.

"Will!" Gwen scolded as Evie tensed. He tightened his fingers around hers in support. He opened his mouth in their defense, but Evie shook her head slightly. She'd asked him to let her take the lead on this, and he'd honor that.

For the moment, anyway.

Will's face was red as he pushed to his feet, every inch the outraged parental figure. "If he married her thinking…"

"He didn't," Evie interrupted, an edge to her voice. "He

didn't know how much I was worth when we met, and when he did find out, he signed my prenup without hesitation. Nick has his own money, Will. He doesn't need mine."

"Everyone needs that kind of money." Evie's brother looked directly at him as he spoke, and Nick bristled at the insult. "At least you thought far enough ahead to have a prenup."

"I'm not stupid, Will."

"*That* seems debatable at the moment."

*Okay, that crossed a line.* "Now just wait—"

Evie interrupted him, holding up a hand. "Stay out of this, Nick."

This was the fight he'd seen her steeling herself for in the elevator. He had to admire her chutzpah; she'd known her brother would react like this—not that he didn't understand where Will was coming from—and yet she hadn't chickened out and simply called with the news. In a strange, train-wreck kind of way, the showdown was fascinating to watch.

Will crossed his arms over his chest. "Who wrote your prenup?"

Evie mirrored the movement. "Sabine's brother."

"*Jackson* drew up a prenup for you and didn't tell me?"

"Well, it's not really your business, now is it, Will?"

"The hell it's not."

Both Harrison siblings were on their feet now and the volume was rising. He was getting hard-pressed not to get involved, regardless of Evie's wishes. Based on Gwen's reaction, though, he didn't jump in the middle. She seemed strangely calm, as if these kinds of fireworks were commonplace.

"Are you pregnant?"

Evie paled at her brother's question. *"What?"*

"I can't think of a single good reason otherwise for you to elope like this. To someone you barely know."

"Maybe I'm just a romantic at heart, swept off my feet by love," she responded.

Nick had never seen someone's head actually explode, but Will had to be close as his voice dropped dangerously. "Evangeline…"

"William…" Evie gritted out.

Gwen cleared her throat. "Voices, please."

Without a word, but still glaring daggers at each other, Will and Evie went out onto the balcony and shut the door. He could no longer hear their battle, but it was certainly still raging. So much for thinking her family was *normal*. Gwen seemed unperturbed by what was going on outside.

She patted him on the shoulder. "Don't worry. Neither of them will end up over the balcony rail. They're volatile, but not homicidal."

"They do this a lot?" He couldn't keep the shock out of his voice.

"Will's a bit overprotective of Evie, and she's always chafed against that. When you throw in that Harrison temper they both have…well, it can get explosive."

*Still…* He could see Evie's wild gesticulations and Will's increasingly deepening frown. Will didn't seem like the kind of man who would take a swing at a woman, but at this point he wasn't sure about anything as far as Evie's family was concerned.

Gwen's eyes followed his to the balcony. "It was hard for me to watch at first, too. It still is, but I understand them both better now. I don't like the boys to hear it, though, so they take it outside. Can I refresh your drink?"

This family was truly nuts. Gwen was playing gracious hostess while Evie and Will fought it out on the balcony. He'd witnessed plenty of violence growing up, and it usually started with people shouting at each other much like Evie and Will were. Rich people—those so-called "good families"—weren't supposed to have that problem. Maybe that was a myth. But he'd be damned if he was going to stand here…

He moved for the glass door, but Gwen stayed him with her hand on his arm.

"They need to get it out, Nick. I promise you, she's fine." Gwen's eyes darkened in understanding, and her voice turned serious. "Really, she's perfectly safe out there. Will has never raised a hand to Evie—*would* never." She led him away from the door, explaining the whole time. "Evie is probably the only person in the world who will go nose-to-nose like that with Will. And, oddly, I think they both enjoy it. I do know that they won't be able to discuss anything like adults until they get *this* out of their systems. They fight fair, though. Don't worry about that." She cocked her head. "I can't believe Evie didn't warn you."

"She did. Sort of." He wondered what else Evie hadn't fully prepared him for. But Gwen didn't have that scared-rabbit look most women wore when they knew someone was about to get hit and were powerless to stop it. If anything, she looked exasperated. That relieved his mind a little.

"Why don't you tell me a little about yourself while we wait? I'll admit I'm terribly curious. Evie's very picky and wouldn't marry just anyone, so you must be something very special. What do you do in Las Vegas?"

This was surreal, but he tried to keep up his end of the conversation while keeping one eye on the balcony. "I run nightclubs."

Gwen beamed. "Oh, Evie should enjoy that."

Here was a chance to learn a few things about his new wife. Like how *much* she loved the nightlife. "Why?"

"Well, she does love to dance, but she had to give up club-bing a couple of years ago just because the press gave her so much grief over it."

He bit back the remark he wanted to make. "She has men-tioned that."

"Evie does her best to avoid the limelight whenever

possible, but that's just not possible for someone like her. Not here, at least. I'm glad you two met in Vegas—you've been allowed a little privacy at least." Gwen leveled a steady look at him. "How *did* you two meet?"

The question was simple enough and her tone was simply curious, but that steady look carried weight. Will might have exploded loudly, but Gwen's inner Mama Bear looked eager to eat him alive if necessary. He tried to put himself in their place and not take offense. It was getting harder by the moment, though.

Evie had wanted to handle this part of the conversation, as well—something else she'd asked for while they were getting their story straight—but since she was occupied at the moment... "Evie came into one of my clubs."

"And it was love at first sight?" Gwen sighed, but he wasn't about to believe he'd tamed the bear that easily. "How romantic. Evie never mentioned a word about what happened on her little Vegas getaway."

He nodded toward the balcony. "I'm not surprised."

Evie chose that moment to pull the door open. She was flushed and her eyes were snapping, and she blew her hair out of her face with a deep sigh. "Will's being a—" She stopped abruptly as her nephews came into the room. "He's, um...I think he needs a little time to calm down, so we'll just go now."

Gwen shook her head. "Leaving me to listen to it? Gee, thanks, Evie."

"Hey, you *chose* to live with the big—*ahem,* with him. I'll call you tomorrow, okay?" Evie hugged Gwen and her nephews, and her face twisted when she looked out on the balcony where her brother stood looking out over the city, the tension in the man's shoulders evident even from where they were. "Tell *him* he can call me when he's ready to admit I'm not fifteen anymore."

With that, Evie grabbed his hand and led him out.

Dear Lord, he hoped insanity wasn't hereditary.

*Why* did Nick keep looking at her as if she'd grown an extra head? She *had* warned him her brother wouldn't take the news well.

Just this once, she'd hoped Will would be able to keep a lid on his temper—especially in front of company. Oh, *no*, that would be too easy. She'd prepared for the worst, but hoped it wouldn't be necessary. It wasn't the first time she'd been wrong. As she pushed the button for the elevator, she turned to Nick. "Sorry about that. I love my brother, but I'd also love to strangle him at the moment."

One of Nick's eyebrows quirked up. "The feeling seemed to be mutual."

She leaned against the elevator wall, trying to look unconcerned as they made their descent, but the energy of the fight with Will was still thrumming through her veins, making her antsy and itchy.

"He pegged the pregnancy, though."

"That was a lucky guess. And I didn't confirm it." Nick still looked at her as if she was an alien, and it was starting to grate across her nerves. Not that she needed much help there; between his attitude of the last twenty-four hours—God, had it really only been twenty-four hours since Nick had shown up at her hotel?—and the still-unresolved fight with Will, her nerves were raw and ready for a fight.

"I'll drive," Nick told the valet when he tried to hand Evie her keys, and Mike looked at her for confirmation. Nick's jaw tensed as he repeated the statement. "You're in no shape to operate heavy machinery at the moment."

Although *she'd* known Mike for three years and Mike didn't know Nick from Adam's house cat, her keys were now in Nick's hand, and Mike was holding the passenger door open for her.

Who the hell did Nick think he was? This was *her* car, her *town,* and he…

Nick revved the engine of her Mercedes. "Are you getting in?"

Mike and the other doormen were watching the exchange with undisguised interest. Evie bit her tongue until she tasted blood to keep from ripping into the lot of them—starting with Nick. *Private matters stay private:* she could hear Gwen's voice in her head, and she let that calm voice be her guide.

Once they got home, though…

"Do you even know where you're going?" she snapped as Nick pulled into traffic.

"I paid attention on the way over. I can handle it. Why are you so testy?"

*Because everyone is trying to run my life for me.* "Switching to decaf is tougher than it sounds."

Nick looked at her oddly before he switched lanes and accelerated around a truck. She turned her head and stared out the window. The familiar sights of Dallas seemed alien, as if everything had been swapped out overnight with something different. But the "something different" in the equation was her.

She was married to a stranger, pregnant with his baby, fighting with her brother—*again*—and her attempts to bring her life under control were only causing it to spiral faster out of hand.

Maybe Will had been right: maybe she did need a keeper. *No,* she didn't. She lifted her chin as the self-pity that was starting to creep in was pushed back by anger and determination. Her life in Dallas was the least of her problems, as it was about to take a backseat anyway to far more pressing issues.

Like moving to Las Vegas. Becoming a mother.

Figuring out the silent man beside her.

Was the Nick she'd met and flipped for—flipped enough to have a fling with, at least—the real Nick? Even with his dangerously rough edges, he'd been fun and exciting and easy to get along with. *That* was the Nick she'd thought she was marrying; in fact, *that* was the reason she'd thought this was a good idea in the first place.

Or was this darkly brooding Nick the real thing? Even allowing for some initial shock time, she wasn't seeing any *real* signs of adjustment that would lead her to believe his attitude would level off into something more acceptable. Or easier to live with.

For a few moments, though, when they'd been at Will and Gwen's, she'd almost felt as if they were a united front. Nick had held her hand and even bowed up those massive shoulders in response to Will's blustering. It had given her a tiny spurt of hope. But Nick's caveman attitude and continuing silence now that they were alone had killed that hope, and she knew the disappointment of *that* was partially fueling her ire at the moment.

The whole thing was giving her a pounding headache, and she couldn't even have a glass of wine to take the edge off.

Nick wasn't lying when he'd said he'd paid attention on the way to Will's, and he never once asked her for directions as he drove. He navigated the tricky entrance to the parking deck under her building with ease and pulled into her assigned parking space without hesitation. He even remembered to insert her key so the elevator would take them up, and the fact he still had her keys instead of giving them back to her irked her even more.

She'd been so deep in thought, due in no small part to his continuing silence, that when he did finally speak to her again, she jumped. "What?"

"I asked you how much of your stuff you were planning to move to Vegas."

"I guess that depends on where I end up living." She reached past him as the elevator doors opened on her floor and pointedly removed *her* key.

"Yesterday, you wanted to move in with me," he said quietly as they walked down the hallway and she opened her condo door.

"Yeah, well, things are a little different now."

"Not worried about your reputation anymore?"

As the door closed behind him, providing them privacy, she let loose some of the frustration that was about to cause her head to explode. "The only people I really care about are Will, Gwen, the boys and Uncle Marcus. Will or Gwen will let Marcus know the news tonight or in the morning, and I'll go see him tomorrow afternoon. The papers will report that I'm married, but once I'm in Las Vegas, no one will really care anymore. Separate living arrangements won't matter since no one in Dallas will know."

Nick leaned against her couch, his face stormy. "And *my* friends?"

"That's your problem, not mine." Tossing her purse and keys onto the table, she went to the kitchen for something cold to drink.

"That's a bit selfish," he challenged.

Her feet froze to the rug, and she bit her lip, trying very hard not to take the bait. She failed. "And you're a bit of a bastard, so this will work out great."

Nick caught up with her in two steps, grabbing her arm and forcing her to look at him. "What the hell is your problem, Evie?"

She was so close to him, she could feel the heat of his skin and see the rapid pulse in his throat. His eyes were dark, though, and she wasn't able to read anything from them. Her body reacted, but she kept her focus. "I could ask you the same question."

Nick's jaw tightened, but the dam was cracked now, and Evie pushed through with a bravado she didn't fully feel. "You obviously have a problem with me. I don't know what it is, and at this point, I'm not sure I really care, but I would like to know one thing—why did you marry me in the first place?"

# CHAPTER SEVEN

EVIE THREW THE QUESTION DOWN like a gauntlet. Frustration and anger charged the air around her, and her eyes were lit up and snapping. But Nick knew this wasn't all just residual anger from her showdown with her brother looking for an outlet; something else simmered beneath the surface.

Although they'd been in close proximity all day, Evie had been distracted, distant even, and he'd had his own thoughts to occupy him. But now her full attention was focused on him, and his body reacted immediately, his skin tightening and muscles tensing. Evie's spacious living room suddenly felt smaller.

He knew Evie felt it, too, even through the heat of her anger, as the tension in the air shifted and heated in a completely different way.

Color rode high on her cheekbones, and her hair tumbled wildly around her face and shoulders. She took a step back, her feet faltering under her the tiniest bit.

She cleared her throat and tossed her hair out of her face, resolutely lifting her chin. "Well? Why?"

The obvious answer was the easiest. "Because you're carrying my baby."

"That was *my* option to solve *my* problem making it all about me, as you've so helpfully reminded me, but it doesn't explain why you'd marry me when…" She stopped as she bit her lip.

That flush now colored the cleavage swelling gently over the neckline of her shirt, and her breath stuttered when she followed his gaze down. "When what, Evie?"

She shook her head slightly and took another step backward. Her back was almost against the wall now—literally—but she squared her shoulders and met his eyes. "When—based on your attitude—you don't even seem to like me very much," she finished baldly.

Oh, he had a multitude of reasons to support his "attitude," as she called it, but only time would tell how accurate his assessment of her would turn out to be and how they'd work out the details. He knew the importance of timing his battles, and it wasn't time for *that* battle with Evie just yet.

*This* situation, though, demanded his immediate attention. The rush of hot blood under Evie's skin had warmed her perfume, and the heady scent filled his lungs and fired through him every time he inhaled. He took another step toward her, and her eyes widened, the pupils dilating as the sexual tension grew stronger than the anger fueling her. He could tell when her body finally switched gears fully; Evie's breath turned shallow, and a tiny shiver moved over her skin.

"I never said I didn't *like* you." Another small step and only inches separated them. He braced one hand on the wall beside her head, and her breath stopped completely as he ran a finger over her shoulder and down her arm. Her stance loosened as he leaned forward, pressing his hips against her, letting her feel exactly how much he "liked" her at the moment.

"Nick…" Her voice was a husky whisper, the honeyed drawl of his name on her lips fanning the slow burn in his groin into a bright, painful flame.

God, he wanted her. From the first moment he'd touched her, he'd wanted her, and although that want had landed him in one hell of an awkward situation, it didn't affect the way Evie heated his blood. And regardless of how they ended up here, the primal part of his brain wouldn't let go of the fact they were married, that Evie was *his* and he should be taking full advantage of that fact.

"Nick…I…I mean, we…shouldn't…um…" Her body contradicted her words as it moved ever-so-slightly against his, her breasts rubbing against his chest, her hips returning the pressure against his straining zipper. Her breath hitched slightly, and a second later her mouth met his.

The force of Evie's raw hunger stole the air from his lungs as her arms locked around his neck and she pulled him fully, possessively, against her. His other hand went to the wall for support, caging Evie between his body and the wall as he ground his hips and felt her shudder in response.

Her taste intoxicated him, leaving him light-headed and craving more. He moved his lips to the column of her neck, causing her to moan low in her throat, and the vibration rippled over his skin. Evie's foot rubbed against his calf, bringing her knee up to nudge at his hip. He slid a hand under her thigh, around to the curve of her bottom, and lifted. Evie's legs twined around his waist like a sinful promise, her head falling back against the wall, giving him access to the cleft between her breasts.

She hissed as his tongue moved over the smooth skin. A quick tug on the thin straps of her shirt at her shoulders, and her breasts were bare, allowing him to pull a nipple into his mouth. Evie arched as his tongue moved over the hard point, and her fingernails dug into his shoulders.

*Sweet mercy.* Evie didn't know whether to shout or cry at the sensations Nick caused. He felt heavenly; the hard heat of his body locked firmly—blissfully—between her thighs while his mouth…oh, *God,* his mouth…

Her brain was a mess of conflicting thoughts—she still wanted to hit Nick with something hard, but at the same time she wanted to finish their fight and get some truths out into the open. But neither hurt pride nor anger—as strong as they were—could hold up against the overwhelming, aching *need* that had hold of her.

*This* was what got her into this predicament in the first place, and letting it sweep her away again was just asking for more trouble she didn't need right now. But her brain wasn't in control right now; her body was, and it was quite sure what it wanted.

*Nick.*

There was too much fabric, too many layers, separating them. She craved skin-to-skin contact, and the constriction of their clothes was maddening.

Nick seemed to share her frustration. His hands worked busily at clasps and buttons, but it wasn't enough. It wasn't fast enough, and she'd go insane if she didn't touch him soon.

With a groan, Nick pushed away from the wall and carried her easily, never once breaking the connection of his lips on hers. She expected the cool softness of her bed to be the next stop, but Nick only took her as far as the table, setting her on the lacquered wood surface and pressing her back with the weight of his body.

A second later, he broke the kiss long enough to sweep her shirt up and over her head, sending it sailing. A tug and her bra was gone. His shirt joined hers on the floor, and she finally had the contact she craved.

Crisp hairs tickled her nipples, teasing the sensitive skin and shrinking her awareness of the world to just the two of them and the tidal wave of pleasure that threatened to engulf her. The slide of denim down her legs barely registered, but the hot sweep of Nick's hands over her calves and thighs had her hands shaking as she tried to work the snap of his jeans. She only had a second to run her hands over the smooth skin of his hips appreciatively before Nick's tongue dipped into her navel to tease and traced a slow, teasing path down to her core.

She arched as he tasted her, and her hands searched futilely for purchase on the slick tabletop. Nick's hands held her hips, and she closed her fingers around his wrists, anchoring them both as he pushed her toward her climax.

When she got there, the explosion shook her to the marrow of her bones, forcing his name out in a cry as she rode the shockwave.

Then Nick was over her, *in* her with a powerful thrust that kept the wave from abating. His fingers twined through hers, pinning her to the table, as Nick set the rhythm and she matched it.

Those deep dark eyes met hers and held her captive, the intimacy of eye contact startling her. Even more surprising was, that for the first time since she'd proposed to him, that guarded, slightly snide expression was gone. Instead, she saw only desire—desire for *her.* Her brain tried to tell her it was simply a physical thing—just sex and hormones overcoming anything else—but that rational thought couldn't deflate the feeling that expanded in her chest.

Just before Nick took her over the edge again, she identified that feeling.

It was hope.

The sound of Sabine's ringtone woke her up, and out of habit she reached to the nightstand to retrieve the phone. It wasn't in its normal spot, and that confused her sleep-muddled brain. So did the heavy weight pinning her legs to the bed...

Nick. The weight was Nick's leg, and the memory of last night rushed in in stunning Technicolor detail. The light peeking in around her drapes told her it was late in the morning—later than she normally slept—but considering how Nick had kept her occupied until the wee hours of the morning...

The ringtone blared again, and Evie slid carefully out from under Nick and the duvet. He muttered and rolled over, but didn't wake. She grabbed her robe off the vanity stool and tiptoed quickly to the living room, closing the bedroom door behind her.

She opened the phone to silence the noise and told Bennie to hold on. Setting the phone down, she slipped her arms into the sleeves and knotted the sash. Then she took the phone to the couch and sat, groaning slightly as her hamstrings lodged a late protest against the gymnastics of the night before.

"'Morning, Bennie."

"You got *married?*" Sabine's voice was an octave higher than normal and twice as loud. Evie winced as she held the phone away from her ear.

"I guess good news travels fast. How'd you hear?"

"Will called Jackson this morning raising all kinds of hell over him writing a prenup for you without telling anyone what you were planning. Jackson called me assuming I knew you'd run off to Vegas to get married, and I didn't even know you'd gone back to Vegas at *all.*" Sabine finally paused to breathe, and Evie could hear the hurt creep into her voice. "Why didn't you *tell* me? Why wasn't I there? And exactly *who* did you marry, anyway? Did you and Tucker get back together?"

*Oops.* "Um, no. I married Nick."

"Nick? Who's Nick? Wait—" Sabine sounded incredulous. "Nick, the-guy-you-hooked-up-with-in-Vegas Nick? *That* Nick?"

"That Nick."

"Oh, Evie… *Why?*"

Evie pulled a cushion into her lap and picked at the seam. What to tell Sabine? Bennie wouldn't believe the "love at first sight" line she was feeding her family, simply because Bennie had been there. She'd talked to her almost every single day since then, and Nick hadn't entered their conversation at all.

That left the truth. The truth only she and Nick knew. She could trust Bennie to keep the truth to herself and not go blabbing to the gossip columnists—Evie knew that in her soul; they had too many years of friendship—but at the same time, she didn't want *anyone* to know.

"Evie, talk to me. Something's not right here. I can tell. What is going on?"

"Bennie..."

Sabine's voice dropped to a near whisper. "Are you *pregnant?*"

Will had asked her the same thing, but Bennie asked with concern in her voice, not outrage, and Evie's resolve cracked. "Yeah," she said quietly. "I am."

"And that's why you married Nick?"

"Pretty much." At Sabine's sharp inhale, Evie hurried ahead. "But you can't tell anyone. Promise me you won't. No one knows about the baby yet."

"I figured as much. Will would have mentioned it to Jackson, and Jackson would have said something to me. I can't believe...I mean... Honey, you didn't have to *marry* him just because you accidentally got pregnant. This isn't the Middle Ages. You have—or at least you *had*—other options."

"Nick has the right to know he's a father. The right to know his child. And the baby..." Evie pulled the cushion against her chest and wrapped her arms around it. "The baby deserves to have a father in its life." That much she was sure of; ethically, she'd done the right thing by Nick and the baby both. It gave her *something,* a piece of moral high ground to stand on.

"All of which could have been achieved *without* getting married." Sabine had a wide practical streak and wasn't one to romanticize anything. "Evie, you barely know him. How could you tie yourself permanently to someone you knew for two measly days?"

No, she couldn't tell Sabine *that* part of the truth. Not right now. The fact this was temporary, just a business arrangement, left a bad taste in her mouth as it was. Thinking about it after the night she'd spent in Nick's arms…that just turned her stomach.

"It's not like there's anyone here I had hopes of marrying one day." *That much was true.* "I like Nick, and we get along great—" she nearly choked on that lie "—and I'm sure things are going to work out great for us. Once I get settled in, we'll—"

"Excuse me? 'Settled in?'" Sabine's voice took on an edge. "Exactly where are you planning on settling in?"

"Well…" Evie hedged. Will and Gwen seemed to accept her moving as a given—and it had fueled a bit of Will's fit last night—but Bennie had a key piece of knowledge they didn't have…

"You're *not* moving to Las Vegas." She paused. "*Are* you?"

"Well, yeah. It's where Nick lives."

"Nick can move his butt down to Dallas. You can't just pack up and move to Vegas. Your whole life is here."

*An excellent reason right there to run away.* "And Nick's life is in Las Vegas. Plus he has a business to run there. It makes much more sense for me to move there."

Sabine huffed. "You've lost your freakin' mind."

*How right she was. But not about this.* "No, Bennie. I'm doing the right thing. For everyone." Evie forced herself to sound upbeat. "I'm really excited. Nick's wonderful, and I know I've made the right decision here. We may be off to a weird start, but there's a happily-ever-after for me out there."

She just didn't know with whom.

"Evie, are you positive? I'm sure Jackson can untie whatever legal knots need to be untied to get you out of this."

"I'm not in anything I need out of. Thanks, though." She needed to end this conversation before it killed her. "Look, I have a really busy day ahead of me—lots to pack, and I need to go to the office…"

"I'll come help," Sabine offered.

"No!" The last thing she needed was a witness today. Especially a witness who knew her so well, she'd be able to see right through the lie. "I mean, we just got married two days ago. We'd like a little privacy, know what I mean?"

Sabine snorted. "Yeah. I think I do."

Evie had the sinking feeling Sabine understood a little *too* much.

Then Sabine sighed. "Look. Just pack up what you need for the immediate future. Make a list of everything else you want done or sent to you, and I'll take care of it. You have enough on your plate."

Tears burned Evie's eyes. "You're the best, Bennie."

"And don't you forget it. You know I expect to be this baby's godmother, right?"

Evie laughed as she swiped at her eyes. "You bet. 'Bye."

She closed the phone and tossed it aside. Leaning forward, she buried her face in the cushion she held. Dear Lord, there was no end to the lies. But she was hip-deep in it now.

Coffee. Coffee would help her face this day, even if it was decaf. She certainly needed a cup before she had to face Nick. Maybe two. She stood, grabbed her phone so she could call Gwen to take the temperature of things there, and turned.

Nick stood in the doorway, bare-chested and barefoot, his jeans riding low on his hips, looking yummy enough to eat with a spoon and nearly causing her nervous system to overload. But his arms were crossed over his chest, an inscrutable look on his face.

*Damn.*

Evie shouldn't look so tempting first thing in the morning. Her hair was mussed from both sleep and where his hands had tangled in it repeatedly the night before. Without makeup, she looked fresh-faced and exotically innocent, but her eyes were red-rimmed with unshed tears. He'd heard enough of her conversation to catch the general gist, but something her friend said had gotten to her.

She shifted, tightening the belt of her robe and pulling the collar closed. The tiny silky robe barely covered anything; it clung to her curves, stopping midthigh on those long legs.

He'd spent the better part of the night with those legs wrapped around him, trapped between her thighs, and the sensation seemed burned into his memory. The temptation to drag her back to the bedroom was strong, but in the harsh, bright light of day, the intimacy they'd shared last night seemed far away.

Evie pushed her hair back, tucking the mass behind her ears. "'Morning. I'm after coffee. Want some?" A perfectly normal and expected set of sentences, but the slight shake of her hands and the too-careful tone of her voice gave her away.

Evie was a complicated creature. It was hard to believe the same woman who railed at him and called him a bastard last night was now treading so carefully. Evie had helped expand his definitions of great sex, but now she mumbled and blushed like a virgin with regrets the morning after.

As she passed him, he could smell her—the scent of sex, him on her—combined with sleep and sweat and her perfume. The smell rekindled that primal need to take her....

But Evie was smiling at him shyly, guardedly. "Breakfast might be more difficult to produce."

"Just coffee. I'm not much of a breakfast eater."

"Me neither." She cocked her head at him. "Wow. We're so compatible, we're practically soul mates."

His body chose to interpret "compatible" in a different way, and his blood immediately rushed south. But Evie's voice lacked sarcasm or snark; she sounded almost teasing with the statement.

"So what are we going to do with all this privacy you asked Sabine for?"

An eyebrow went up, but the blush that stained her cheeks ruined the effect. "You were eavesdropping?"

"Just enough to hear how wonderful I am," he teased, enjoying the way the blush deepened.

Evie handed him a cup of coffee. "I had to tell Bennie *some*thing."

"Like we got married because you're pregnant."

"Bennie knows me too well to believe it was love at first sight or anything like that." Evie drank and then wrinkled her nose, staring at her cup in distaste. "Ugh. This part of being pregnant is not fun at all."

It was the first time she'd mentioned the physicality of being pregnant, and he realized he'd never asked, either. "Morning sickness?"

She sighed sadly. "Not that. Not yet, at least. It's the lack of caffeine. I don't care what people say—decaf just doesn't taste the same as regular. And facing the day without caffeine just sucks."

"So you've given it up entirely?"

"Caffeine, sushi, Brie, alcohol, pâté…there's a whole list of wonderful stuff I'm not allowed to have anymore. Plus there's a whole list of things I *should* be eating that just doesn't balance out what I'm giving up. It's almost depressing. Oh, and the prenatal vitamins—*yuck*. They're the size of horse pills *and* they stink."

How did Evie know all of this? The question must have shown on his face.

"I did some reading on the plane," she said by way of explanation and dismissed it with a shrug. "By the way, you don't happen to know who's the best obstetrician in Las Vegas, do you? I'll need to get an appointment soon."

"I didn't realize you were so organized." He'd assumed

Evie's actions to this point had all been reactionary, but now it seemed she had put *some* thought into this beyond saving her own reputation.

"I have layers." Her mouth twisted and she lifted her chin. "I just might surprise you."

"You already do." He could tell she didn't know how to respond to that candid statement.

"Ditto."

To be fair, he'd been a little reactionary himself the past couple of days, and that wasn't something he was used to at all. He still had a lot to figure out about Evie and how he wanted this to shake out in the end, but for now... "So what is the plan for today?"

*Go back to bed and stay there* was too much to hope for.

She leaned a hip against the counter, and he mirrored the movement, as if this was just a normal morning chitchat between husband and wife. "Well, I need to go see Uncle Marcus, and I need to check in with Gwen and see if Will is still acting like a butthead about this. I have to call my assistant, and I need to start packing."

Back to the topic that set her off last night. Not that he minded how *that* worked out. But living arrangements did need to be settled. "I assure you my home is fully furnished with all the modern conveniences. But feel free to bring any personal items you'd like to have around. We'll find someplace for them."

"I don't know..."

"Your original plan involved you moving in. And it does make sense. I have plenty of room, and it will be much easier in the long run." *Right.* And he'd be able to keep an eye on her and the baby.

Evie frowned as her hands went to the collar of her robe again, pulling the edges even farther over each other. In light of last night, she had to be thinking about her earlier plan to just be roommates. But last night had changed the game.

Even if she hadn't figured it out by now, *that* idea was out of the question. If Evie was moving to Vegas, she was moving in with him.

And if she was moving in, she was moving into his bedroom.

# CHAPTER EIGHT

EVIE DIDN'T RECALL SIGNING a treaty or even participating in peace talks, but she and Nick seemed to have called a cease-fire. A truce of sorts.

Which should have made her happy, especially since Uncle Marcus had called with an invitation to lunch—and there was no way to get out of an "invitation" from Uncle Marcus—in order to meet "her young man," and it was just too nerve-racking to play happy couple when Nick looked at her as if… Well, as if there was something *wrong* with her.

But it was an uneasy, superficial truce—at least for her, because the only thing that was different from yesterday was the completely mind-scrambling sex they'd had last night.

It was hardly what relationship experts would suggest as a way to broker peace, but somehow, it had worked. Some-what. Nick wasn't being overly friendly, but he was less monosyllabic today. He wasn't quite the same man who'd shifted her out of her usual orbit in Vegas, but he wasn't that same cold-eyed man she'd left the wedding chapel with, either. Somewhere in the middle was the man who'd done things she didn't think were humanly possible to her body last night and made her love every minute of it.

And yet this morning…well, it was weird, to say the least. Neither of them mentioned last night. Or the future. Or anything really. Their conversation had been well, not *easy,* but not difficult, either. It had been a surprisingly simple morning full of surprisingly normal conversation like "Would you like the shower first?" and "What channel is ESPN?"

It was nerve-racking at the same time it was oddly comforting, but in the grand scheme of things *that* was still a major improvement.

More importantly, it had made lunch a little easier. Uncle Marcus was buying their story, and Nick seemed to be passing this interview with flying colors. She tried to feign interest in their spirited discussion of...what? Mutual funds? *Seriously?* At least it was something.

It still bothered her a lot, though, that the *one* thing Nick did seem to like about her was how good she was in bed.

For one, it would mean she had completely misjudged Nick—both when she'd made the decision to sleep with him in the first place and again when she'd decided to marry him. She didn't want to think she was that naive. Or so easily blinded by her hormones.

"You're not eating, Evangeline. Is there something wrong with your salad, my dear?"

Uncle Marcus's question snapped Evie back to the conversation. Damn, her brooding over Nick had caused her to forget where she was. Uncle Marcus might be closing in on eighty and his heart problems had left his body frail, but he still had the ability to make her feel like an uncouth tomboy with little more than a pointed stare.

"No, Uncle Marcus, it's delicious. I'm just rather tired today. I didn't get much sleep last night."

Nick coughed slightly, and she cursed herself silently as she added, "Between all the traveling and then dealing with Will yesterday... Well, you know."

Marcus nodded. "Oh, I got an earful from William this

morning, but I'll be sure to let him know that your Nicolas seems to be on the up-and-up and not at all a gold digger."

Evie bit her lip as Nick stiffened at the label. Nick had borne Uncle Marcus's pointed and unrelenting interrogation—however cloaked in politeness it was—with a restraint and patience she admired and envied.

Now, in typical Uncle Marcus fashion, he seemed to believe that his stamp of approval—or disapproval—marked the end of all discussions on the topic. She could wish, but she and Will still had a conversation on the horizon. Patting Nick on the arm, where she could feel the tightened muscle, she smiled at Uncle Marcus. "Thank you. Will trusts your judgment so much, I'm sure that will go a long way in easing his mind about our marriage. I know this caught him off guard."

"You must realize, Evangeline, this has caught all of us off guard." His mouth curled just the slightest bit down in disapproval. "I still don't see why you had to run off to Las Vegas for some quickie wedding, when we've looked forward to your wedding day for so long."

*Oh, let's not go there.* "I know, Uncle Marcus." She tried to sound appropriately contrite. "But you know sometimes I just get caught up in things." Her cheeks were hurting from the smile she'd worn for the last hour, but she forced herself to keep it up and just prayed it looked like sincere excitement. "Nick kind of swept me off my feet."

"I had hoped you had outgrown your occasional penchant for the dramatic by now. It embarrasses the family and the company when those dramatics hit the papers."

*Ouch.* Uncle Marcus sure knew how to score a direct hit on her conscience. As if he somehow felt her inner wince, Nick took her hand. Everyone else might see it as newlywed-itis, but she took it as a much-needed pillar of support. If only Uncle Marcus knew how she was trying so desperately *not* to embarrass everyone with even more drama....

"I'm afraid I'm to blame for this," Nick interjected and she nearly choked. "Evie's spontaneity is part of her charm, and I encouraged her more than I should have."

She couldn't believe her ears. Nick was defending her?

"I'm not accustomed to the level of attention Evie attracts," he continued as she tried to hide her shock behind her water glass. "I hoped an elopement would make a quick splash and be forgotten, whereas planning a big white wedding would draw endless amounts of attention. I don't like the idea of being fodder for the society columns."

She was still reeling from that statement, but when Uncle Marcus nodded in agreement, it took everything she had to keep her jaw from hitting the table in shock. Her world spun off its axis, and she could only hope her eyes weren't bugging out of her head as Nick and Uncle Marcus bonded over the tiresome burden of being grist in the gossip mill.

"That's probably a wise attitude to have, young man. Beat the busybodies at their own game. I've always felt there was far too much speculation about everyone else's personal business going on. Never cared for it, myself."

Evie looked around the room carefully. It was the same dining room where she'd eaten hundreds of lunches the last decade, filled with the same people she'd known for years, yet she felt she'd landed on another planet. She'd love to know exactly when the pod-people had taken over Marcus's body and implanted this new aversion to "what everyone else thinks." She'd spent the last ten years worrying about what everyone else thought and might say—primarily because *Marcus* worried about it so much. In fact, Uncle Marcus was usually the first in line to raise an eyebrow.

Her world was now completely, officially askew.

Did pregnancy cause insanity? Maybe she was caught in some wishful daydream? The hand holding hers felt real enough: warm and strong and just calloused enough to remind her he wasn't a pretty boy with a desk job at his daddy's firm. And the way his other hand was sliding over her forearm…gooseflesh rose behind the feather-light touch.

No, this was real. Weird, but real. That cautious bubble of optimism inflated in her chest again. She had three people on her side—Bennie, Gwen and now Uncle Marcus. Between the three of them, they'd have the gossip columns under control, and eventually, they'd get past Will's pigheadedness, too.

Which meant she only had Nick to deal with. And, for now at least, they had a truce. She might not like how that truce came about, but she was rapidly learning to take what she could get. She'd build on what she had and go from there.

It wasn't *that* bad of a start. At least half her plan was working out. A little voice in her head, though, wouldn't stop wishing the half that was working out already was the half that involved Nick.

Evie lived in a very strange world, Nick decided. Lunch with her Uncle Marcus—who must have been from a different branch of the family tree—had driven that point home.

In all honesty, her family's reaction wasn't unexpected considering Evie's inheritance and the fact she was the youngest and obviously doted on. But it was the last two hours that had him shaking his head at the world Evie inhabited.

It started when they arrived at the country club and a person stepped in front of them to snap off a photo before the doorman shooed the cameraman away.

"What was that?" he asked.

Evie shrugged. "That's Malcolm Wilson. Amateur paparazzo. You just made the 'Texas High-Life' blog. Congrats."

"Because I'm here?"

"Because you're here with *me*." A tentative smile crossed her face. "I did warn you. People are interested in my family."

Belatedly, he realized that now included him. Great. "Why?"

"Because we have money? Because we're considered influential? Maybe Dallas doesn't have enough real celebrities? I don't know for sure why, but it comes with the territory. If I got all bent out of shape every time someone took my picture and posted it somewhere…" She shrugged again. "Let's just say I don't leave the house without makeup."

Still reeling from that, he'd borne Evie's uncle's interrogation with all the patience he could muster, drawing on his last reserves when Evie sent him a grateful look and squeezed his hand.

But what really had him shaking his head had nothing to do with paparazzi or elderly relatives. In two hours at the country club—and the majority of that spent at a table with her uncle—no fewer than fourteen people had waylaid them. He'd expected some of it, simply because this was Evie's family's club and she was bound to know a lot of people, but these hadn't been fourteen simple "Hi-how-ya-doin" quick conversations.

Some knew of their marriage already, causing Evie to mumble something about Gwen being quick to the punch this morning with all the appropriate spin, but even he could tell people were fishing for details. Evie deftly deflected the questions without once losing her smile or seeming ungracious in any way.

He was more impressed, though, at how easily Evie handled the requests for her time or her money for everyone's various pet projects. He dealt with his fair share of that at home—and it was getting worse every day as his bank balance grew—but he could tell Evie had lots of practice in this area, as well.

In many ways, Evie was a different person in Dallas. Her smile was brighter but less genuine, and she seemed more reserved than he remembered—and it couldn't be him causing it. It took him a little while—about five or six sets of introductions and conversations—to figure it out.

These were superficial relationships; they were far more

interested in what she could do for them than how she was. No wonder she didn't want these people to know she'd gotten pregnant accidentally; they'd eat her alive and relish every bite.

And the reason why she often spoke of "Evangeline Harrison" as if she was a different person became clear. Evie had a role to play, and she played it well. No matter how much it chafed against her true personality.

But what was her true personality? He needed to remember who she was, not be blinded to the truth and how women like Evie could be. He needed to keep that reminder front and center.

So another piece of the Evie puzzle fell into place, but it still was far from a complete picture. No wonder she'd run off to Vegas to blow off steam. And no wonder she was so willing to move there now that she had an excuse. But was Vegas where she'd want to stay? Did she need all of this—as superficial as it was?

Her polite smile didn't falter until they were safely inside the car and he eased the car out of the club's driveway. She blew out her breath noisily as she leaned back against the seat. "Well, that wasn't so bad."

"You expected worse?"

"I always expect the worst. It helps keep my mouth in check, and curbs that penchant for the dramatic that bothers Uncle Marcus so much." Her mouth twisted. "The family's image, by the way, used to be Marcus's number-one thing. I don't know *who* that man was, telling you your private life was none of anyone's business."

Evie sounded so grumpy about it, he couldn't help but laugh, and she shot him a dirty look for it.

Casually, as if he wasn't fishing for information, he asked, "Is he as tough on his own kids, or are you the only dramatic Harrison in the clan?"

"There aren't many Harrisons in the clan. Will and I are the only ones—plus Gwen and the boys, of course. But Will doesn't make the papers much since he married Gwen, and the boys are too young, so I'm the only one they're interested in right now. Uncle Marcus is a committed bachelor, and if he has any family at all, I've never met them."

*Wait.* He'd been through a military-grade interrogation and the man wasn't even a true relative? "You mean Marcus isn't really your uncle?"

"No. He and my father were great friends, and he's been with the company since the earth's crust cooled. He kind of adopted our family, but I didn't really know him until I moved back here."

It was slightly shocking how little he knew about Evie personally, especially since he knew so much about her *physically*. At the same time, they hadn't had much time to really talk, and this was the most open and approachable Evie had been since she left Vegas the first time. He needed to take advantage of it. "I assumed you grew up in Dallas."

"No. I was born here, but we moved away when I was five. I told you how Will had to take me in after my mom died, right? I came back to Dallas when I was fifteen." She laughed, but it was a slightly bitter sound. "It was a huge adjustment because I just walked into the fishbowl and was totally unprepared for any of it. That's a whole different story, but that's what Uncle Marcus is talking about when he mentions my 'penchant for dramatics.'"

He could almost feel sorry for her, growing up under a spotlight like that. But then he thought of Evie up on the stage at Starlight…if she was that free and adventurous in a strange place around strangers, what kind of trouble did she stir up in her hometown?

Maybe the reserve he'd seen recently was unusual for her, a by-product of the situation. Evie obviously knew what was expected of her—today was proof of that—but if her family was on her case a lot, it had to be deserved. When he'd researched her family briefly just to get a feel for what he would be walking into, maybe he should have read past the who-wore-what-where.

He should've been looking closely for clues, information to tell him how much Evie and his mother had in common....

"It's funny, you know," Evie continued, unaware of his brief lapse of attention. "Gwen is the etiquette expert, so you'd think she'd be the one to really worry about, but Uncle Marcus is the real stickler. I love him, but…"

"And your brother?"

"What about him?"

"Does he agree with Marcus about your 'dramatics'?"

"Will doesn't care so much that it ends up being news, if you understand my meaning. He doesn't like the gossip, but it's not the gossip that bothers him. Uncle Marcus focuses on the gossip, while Will is more focused on *me*."

"That sounds like a pain. Especially after what I saw last night."

She shook her head. "Don't worry about last night. Will's a lot of bark, and he tends to forget I'm an adult now, but he'll come around. He always does." She sounded sure of that.

"*Always?* You've eloped before?"

"No, like I said, this is definitely the *biggest* stunt I've pulled, but it's not the first. And it won't be the last."

"Planning to rob a bank or something?" Even with all his doubts and questions about Evie, he was still enjoying himself. She was certainly entertaining.

"Nope, just giving birth barely nine months after the wedding and then getting a divorce. It's gonna be fun," she added sarcastically. "That will make everyone's head explode."

"So why bother with getting married?"

"Because divorce is too common to be hugely newsworthy. It will get reported, dissected and speculated about, but ultimately, that's a family matter very few people can throw stones about."

Evie might end up in the press a lot, but she also had a savvy understanding of it. "Great. I'll have your big brother coming after my hide."

"I'm pretty sure you can hold your own against Will."

Oddly, he took that as a compliment.

Lowering her voice, she added conspiratorially, "And if it comes down to a fistfight, I got a fifty on you."

Was she teasing him? This was definitely a different Evie, reminiscent of Las Vegas. He feigned affront. "Only a fifty? Your brother's got… What? Twenty years on me?"

"Hmm… From what I saw on our marriage license—and happy belated birthday, by the way—it's closer to fifteen. But you *do* have all that experience in bar fights…. Still, I think a fifty is a safe bet." She grinned broadly at him, turning the charm on high.

"If you're going to live in Las Vegas, we need to work on your betting skills. You'll never make any money that way."

Evie laughed. "Not everyone gambles because they need the money. They gamble for the thrill."

Very true. And that knowledge would help her immensely in acclimating. "You checked out my birthday on the marriage license?"

"I was curious." She thought for a minute, then added, "I figured since we were getting married, I should at least know your birthday and middle name."

He pretended he needed to concentrate to navigate the entrance to the parking deck as a stall for time. Evie must really think he was a first-class bastard if she wasn't willing to ask even the simplest of questions. "Those aren't state secrets."

"Well…" Evie looked at him over the rims of her sunglasses. "You're not exactly Mister-hey-ask-me-anything."

How many times had Kevin said much the same thing?

That's why he and Kevin made a good team—Kevin could do all the talking so he didn't have to. Unfortunately, Kevin wasn't here to answer Evie's questions for him. "Try me."

She fell silent and he could almost see the gears turning in her head. She must be coming up with something really…

"What's your favorite color?"

All that thought for *that?* "Black."

"I'm not surprised. It's a good color for you. Do you listen to country music?"

*This* was Evie's idea of getting to know each other? His earlier hopes of Evie's depths were being quickly battered down. "No."

"Umm…favorite movie?"

*"Shaun of the Dead."*

"Really?" Her mouth dropped in disbelief.

"Really. It's a great movie. Next question."

He pulled into her parking space and killed the engine. Evie didn't wait for him to open her door or hold out her hand for her keys. He couldn't decide if that was a good thing or not.

She fired her next question as they waited for the elevator. "Cats or dogs?"

"Neither. I'm never home. But you can get one if you like after you settle in."

A wistful smile flashed briefly. "How about hobbies?"

He fought to keep a straight face. "I collect stamps."

Evie's eyes grew wide and her mouth fell open. "You're kidding me."

"Of course I am." He rubbed his arm where Evie smacked him. "Seriously, Evie, *these* are the burning questions you have for me?"

She fiddled with her purse. "I'm trying to get to know you. Since we're going to be living together…"

"At least that's settled."

"Did I have much of a choice?" she challenged, an edge creeping into her voice.

He tried to dull the edge from his own voice even though she was trying his nerves again. Evie barely clutched before she shifted gears. "It's a free country. I can't force you to do anything."

She snorted as he opened the door to her apartment, and she passed him to go inside. She hung her bag on the back of a chair and leaned her hips against the table. Evie frowned as she ran a hand over a large smudge on the shiny finish.

Her handprint. The image of Evie on her back, her hair spilling over the table and off the edge, slammed into him, and he no longer cared about silly get-to-know-you questions. The most important knowledge was that the bedroom was only steps away.

He knew the moment Evie realized what caused that smudge. She jumped up as if she'd been burned. "Wh-what were we talking about? Um… Oh, yeah, um, getting to know each other."

Evie moved busily around the room, avoiding eye contact as she straightened magazines and fluffed cushions.

"Then it's my turn now to ask you some questions."

She cleared her throat. "Of course. My favorite color is blue, and I like dogs and *The Sound of Music*…"

Evie might be willing to waste her Q&A time on shallow topics, but he didn't have that kind of patience. He needed some answers—some truths—and now was as good a time as he was likely to get. "Those were your questions. Not mine."

"Oh. Right."

And there was that unexpectedly quick shift in gears. From teasing, to turned on, to nervous in less than a minute. Now she squared her shoulders, took a deep breath and switched gears again. Hands behind her back and chin up, she faced him as if he was a firing squad. As if she read his thoughts, she smiled weakly. "Fire away."

*Why* did Nick make her so nervous? She felt like a babbling fool half the time—make that *most* of the time—she tried to have a conversation with him. He'd handed her the golden opportunity to ask him all the questions she'd been storing up, and she'd chickened out. She wanted to know, *really* know, this enigmatic man she'd married, but she'd defaulted to stupid questions instead because she was a coward.

Even worse, she had the feeling he knew it.

Oh, and the look on his face when she'd noticed the smudgy handprint on her table. That only made it worse, because it reminded her how she'd ended up here. How much she wanted him to like her for something more than...*ugh*. For something *more* than how they ended up here.

God, she was pathetic. For a minute there, she'd let herself believe their act; that what they were presenting to Will and Gwen and Uncle Marcus and the rest of Dallas had even a grain of truth in it.

It was just too easy to lose sight of the reality of their situation when faced with a memory like last night. How Nick made her feel as if... As if this could be real. Even if it wasn't.

His voice was hard. "What made you decide to marry me? And what would you have done if I'd said no?"

Nick obviously didn't have the same yellow streak running through him that she'd recently discovered in herself. He went straight for the tough questions. The kind she didn't have the guts to ask when they weren't shouting at each other, and she had an actual chance of getting an answer.

"I decided to marry you for the same reason you decided to marry me. I'm carrying your baby. It's pretty straightforward." She took a deep breath and squeezed her fingers together. "And, honestly, I didn't have a backup plan."

"Because you always get what you want?" There was that mocking tone again.

*If he only knew.* "Hardly. It just didn't occur to me that you'd say no. You seemed like a decent, upstanding guy who'd want to do the right thing for his child—however unplanned it was."

That earned her a skeptical look. "Exactly how did you come to this great understanding of my psyche? We didn't do a whole lot of talking."

"Just a feeling I had. But look," she said, trying to sound upbeat, "I was right. And here we are."

A black eyebrow arched up. "And you don't think this is an enormous mistake?"

*All the time. Definitely every time you look at me like that.* That eyebrow, though… It infuriated her at an elemental level she didn't quite understand. And his tone. He was just like—

*Will.* A clarity she wished she'd had much earlier settled on her shoulders.

Oh, *damn it.* After ten years of butting heads with her brother, somehow she'd managed to find a man just like Will. And she *married* him, for goodness' sake. No wonder…

Dear God, she needed some *serious* therapy.

But if she could handle her brother… Something inside her solidified, and she found her backbone again. It felt good. "Is it?" she challenged. "You tell me."

Nick's other eyebrow joined the first at his hairline, and the shock on his face made her feel much better. Like herself again. She might be Evie Rocco now, but she was still Evangeline Harrison, damn it, and it was high time she remembered that. "Well? Are you going to make me regret this?"

"Me? It was your idea."

"Yes, you keep reminding me of that, thank you. But no one forced you to the altar at gunpoint. Why is that, Nick? You've made it very clear that this wasn't your idea, *and* that you don't think it was a very good choice, yet you agreed pretty quickly." Oh, she was really getting warmed up now. "Why, Nick? Was it the money? My family's connections? Planning on expanding to Dallas and figured you could get your foot in the door?"

She was goading him, trying to force him to react, hoping he'd drop a bit of that shield and answer her with some honesty. Nick's face reddened in anger and his jaw locked, but he didn't take the bait quite the way she hoped. His voice was dangerously quiet and mocking as he said, "It had nothing to do with your money, Evie. It was all about you."

Her heart jumped in her chest, an involuntary reaction to his words before the tone fully registered and squashed the feeling.

"I know your type, Evie. Vegas is full of women just like you—rich, beautiful..." He sneered the word, killing the compliment as he stalked toward her. "But spoiled and out only for a good time. Their children make great accessories—until they don't anymore, and then they're an inconvenience. I won't let that happen to my child."

She held her ground as he got closer and his voice grew even more mocking. "It's very simple, Evie. Marrying you gave me legal rights to my child—rights I couldn't be guaranteed as easily otherwise. You aren't the only one able to make plans, Evie. Marrying you won't be a mistake—at least not for me. You might come to regret it, but I assure you I won't, because I'm getting *exactly* what I wanted out of this."

His words punched her stomach like hard fists, and she wanted to curl into a ball to protect herself—and the baby, too—from such ugliness. She didn't doubt the truth of the words; she pushed and goaded to get the truth out of him and now she had it.

In her anger, she'd made a tactical error: she couldn't handle Nick the way she handled Will, and she shouldn't have tried. Will loved her and acted only in her best interest—however misguided he was about that interest. Nick didn't like her, had his own interests to protect, and she'd just backed herself into a very bad corner.

Oh, yes, she'd made a huge mistake. And now she couldn't find her tongue to say anything at all.

Nick looked her up and down with hot eyes before shaking his head and walking out the door. The sound of the slamming door echoed through her apartment like a gunshot.

Her knees began to wobble and she found a chair before they gave out entirely. At least she now had a reason for why Nick didn't like her—even if she didn't quite understand why or how or when he'd made such dramatic judgments about her character.

When would she learn to watch her mouth? Just a few minutes ago they were talking about *movies,* and she'd been so hopeful. But now...

What was she going to do now?

# CHAPTER NINE

A TWENTY-MINUTE WALK AROUND Evie's neighborhood helped cool his temper, but now he felt exactly like the bastard Evie accused him of being. For someone Evie had called the strong, silent type, he sure had a big mouth.

He knew he lacked patience, but he'd always managed to keep a lid on his temper—even when his patience was pushed to its limits. It was a point of pride with him as well as a business philosophy. Anger led people to say and do stupid things, and hotheads rarely prevailed.

So where was his trademark silence and self-control when it came to Evie? One toss of her hair and he wanted to bend her over the nearest table. Then she'd grin at him and make him laugh. But that determined and stubborn lift of her chin made him want to strangle her.

Tease to tempt to temper with unbelievable speed and zero warning. He'd learned quickly *she* was capable of those extremes, but finding those extremes in himself? Good Lord. Dealing with Evie was like driving a fast car with no breaks around sharp curves while wearing a blindfold.

No wonder he was losing his mind. There just wasn't another explanation for any of this. Something had to give before they either killed each other or…

Or what?

He and Evie could draw up legal agreements all day long, but those weren't going to be much use in the day-to-day trenches. How was he supposed to create a decent home for his child when he and Evie kept snapping each other's heads off?

And Evie was getting more complicated with each passing minute. Accidentally pregnant or not, Evie had looked rather shocked—and offended—when he matter-of-factly informed her he didn't expect her to be much of a mother. *That* reaction had been real; Evie wasn't that good of an actress. It was such an honest look, he'd almost felt bad for saying it in the first place.

He shouldn't. There was too much riding on this bet.

But he did. It was absolutely infuriating.

To make matters worse, *none* of this did a damn thing to damp the fire that burned in his veins for her. It was insult to injury, salt in the wound, to want a woman *that* much even as she tore through his life like a flash flood.

Even now—not half an hour after he'd stormed out of her apartment—he wanted nothing more than to drag her into her bedroom and bury himself in her for the foreseeable future.

What he needed was to get Evie out of his system. Eventually, he'd get enough of her and the drugging, addictive effect she had on him.

Maybe then, he'd be able to think straight again.

Otherwise, this was never going to work. For any of them.

She simply couldn't go on like this. The stress was tearing her apart—and it couldn't be good for the baby, either. She and Nick had to come to some kind of real understanding, or else she simply wouldn't make it a month—much less a year—without killing him or driving herself insane.

She took several deep breaths, trying to calm herself.

*Work the problem, Evie.* One step at a time. Right now, the problem looked insurmountable and complex, but that was because Nick was at the middle. *Work the bits you can, then. Start at the edges.*

Where had he gone? Her keys were still on the table, so he didn't have access to a vehicle....

*That's not your problem. He's an adult.* He'd come back when he was ready, and hopefully, he would be calmer then. She needed to use this time to get her head together, to formulate a plan. She'd be able to function better if she had some solid ground under her feet. She'd been running on instinct for days now simply trying to mitigate the damages—no wonder she was half-crazy.

Right. Time to make a plan, then.

She dug a legal pad and a pen out of the drawer and pulled a chair up to the table. She tapped the pen against the paper as she tried to focus, but those smudged handprints kept drawing her eyes like a magnet. Muttering a curse, she went to the kitchen, grabbed a dust rag from under the sink and went to work removing the evidence.

It was torture, and it stirred up images she needed *not* to think about if she was going to be able to think straight at all. Her body wasn't getting the message, though. Her pelvic muscles contracted, sending a ripple up through her body until it reached her jaw and made her swallow hard.

*Work the problem, damn it.* Sex wasn't the problem. Well, not one she could really address at the moment. *Focus.*

She drew columns, labeled them and started orderly numbered lists of what she needed to do, what she needed to pack. The lists grew, the numbers moving into double digits, but she pressed on, not letting the length of the list panic her. She even added a couple of things to the list that she could cross off already—like telling Uncle Marcus—just to make herself feel as if she'd accomplished something.

Evie ran her finger over the last item in the list. *Nick.* In reality, he was number one, but she'd refused to think about it until she had everything else down on paper, simply because he was the most complicated and the most likely to overwhelm her if she thought about it too much.

Oddly, though, it didn't overwhelm her. She traced over his name, and a strange serenity settled on her shoulders. She did it again, and the feeling intensified.

This was ridiculous. *He* was the source of all her problems. *He* had just shouted at her and stormed out of her apartment. He didn't even like her, so why on earth was his entry on the list making her feel...

Better?

No, not really better. He brain stuttered and scrambled and butterflies battered her insides when she thought of him. Her heart beat faster and arousal heated her skin. That didn't fall under the category of "better." But there was no mistaking that odd feeling of serenity.

That had to be a good sign for the future. Either that, or she was a glutton for punishment and cracked in the head. She drummed the pen on the table. *Maybe?*

It made no sense at all. Nick was the center of the storm: everything unsettling and destructive in her life swirled around him.

*The eye of the hurricane is the calmest.*

She scrubbed her finger over the shiny surface of the table, leaving a smudge. With just a touch, Nick certainly let loose a hurricane inside *her.* The first time, the intensity had both excited and scared her.

Now she craved that feeling—and that explained a lot.

What it didn't explain was why when Nick touched her, she felt as if she was in the eye of the storm at the same time. The only time these days she felt as if her life *wasn't* spinning completely out of control, threatening to destroy everything and everyone she loved, was when Nick held her.

Evie jumped to her feet at that disturbing thought and began to pace. She *had* lost her mind this time. If not for Nick, her life wouldn't be spinning out of control in the first damn place.

*It's the hormones.* Something biological was causing that feeling. Residual caveman instinct to connect her to the father of the child she carried. Genetic programming from her evolutionary ancestors.

Because if it wasn't... Oh, dear Lord, she was in *big* trouble.

Two hours later, Evie's doorman waved him past the desk and straight to the elevator. Nick had to respect a building that ran with that much efficiency and attention to its residents that they already knew who he was.

He tried the handle of Evie's door before he knocked, and he was surprised to have it open easily under his hand. Either living in a limited-access building had Evie's guard down or else she'd left it unlocked in anticipation of his return. If it was the former, she'd have to break that habit once she moved to Vegas; his neighborhood might be gated, but it was isolated and a tempting target for burglars. If it was the latter...

That was a good sign, right?

Evie was on the couch, her laptop open and a phone pressed to her ear. From the sound of it, she was speaking to someone at her office, tying up loose ends and making arrangements for business to go on without her. She looked up as he closed the door, and ended the call quickly.

Three large suitcases sat next to the door.

With a careful—if slightly forced—pleasantness, Evie said, "You're back."

Good. Evie had cooled down as well and wasn't going to immediately reopen hostilities with an opening shot. He carefully kept his voice level, as well. "Yeah. I spent some time at that Internet café two blocks from here taking care of some business back home."

"Oh. You're welcome to do that here, too. Use the computer…whatever."

He indicated the phone and laptop. "Is that what you were doing? Taking care of business?"

She closed the computer and set it on the coffee table. "Yep. It's all taken care of."

"That was easy."

"Well, Will's been slow to hand over much responsibility to me. It's not that he doesn't trust me, he just still sees me as his little sister and…" She stopped and shrugged. "Most of my job could be done by a well-trained monkey. My assistant is pretty sharp and could easily handle everything, so she just landed a nice promotion. I'll keep a few fingers in a couple of projects while I'm gone and finish up a few things long-distance, but otherwise, I'm now free to do whatever."

An odd smile crossed her face as she spoke. Evie didn't seem upset to be leaving her job at all. Then she nodded at the suitcases. "And I'm pretty much packed, so we can leave whenever you're ready."

This was much quicker than expected. Either Evie was very well-organized or else she was leaving a lot undone. Why the big hurry to leave? "That's all you're taking?"

"I know. It's weird to me, too. I think I took more than that on my last vacation. I'm not normally what you'd call a light packer."

Guilt nagged at him—a new, unusual feeling—that he had implied she shouldn't, or couldn't, bring much with her. "You can bring anything you want with you, Evie. I have plenty of room."

"I know," she quickly interrupted, "and I started to pack all kinds of stuff. Then I realized I didn't know what I would need. I don't even need a lot of clothes, because I'll be outgrowing these soon anyway." She rubbed a hand over her still-flat abdomen. "Sabine or Gwen can mail me anything I decide

I do need, and, in reality, I'm not going to be gone all that long. No sense dragging everything I own to Las Vegas only to move it all back in another year."

Evie sounded upbeat about the move—and the move back. That bothered him more than he liked. He had no doubt her attitude would change, but for the moment, she sounded downright chipper, not something he'd expected to return to after the way he'd left earlier.

"Hey, Evie…"

"Look, Nick," she said at the same time. She stopped and clasped her hands in her lap. "I'm sorry. Go ahead."

"Ladies first."

"Okay." She stood and circled the couch, ending up standing right in front of him. Then Evie set her shoulders and lifted her chin, and he braced himself for another volley. "I'm sorry."

The apology caught him off guard, but Evie didn't seem to notice as she hurried ahead.

"For a lot of things, but primarily for earlier. Well, my attitude has pretty much sucked recently, and I've taken it all out on you. And I am sorry for that." He opened his mouth, but Evie held up a hand. "I really need to say all of this before you respond. You're holding up your end of the bargain admirably, and I can't thank you enough for how you've acted around my family. I'll sleep a lot better and worry a lot less now that I know they're satisfied. Now, I'd really like for us to come to another agreement. One where we don't snipe and yell at each other."

That was quite a speech. She'd been thinking while he was gone. "I think that sounds like an excellent plan."

He didn't realize how forced her pleasantness had been until her shoulders sagged and she laughed. A genuine laugh this time; the one he didn't hear very often. "Thank goodness. I know you might not believe this, but most people say I'm pretty easy to get along with."

Her voice was both earnest and lighthearted at the same time—a combination only Evie could ever manage. "Is that so?"

"Yes, it is," she responded primly. "My only explanation is that this situation has put me under a lot of stress, and I'm learning that I don't handle stress all that well."

Regardless of her light tone, she'd swallowed a lot of her pride to make that speech; it was only fair that he do the same. "It's been stressful for me, too, and I'm learning a similar lesson."

"Oh, good, we're *both* growing as people then. Gwen talks about building and showing character through adversity. I think I've been building a whole cast of characters." Her mouth twisted. "Not all of them are shining stars of the show, though."

Evie's charm; he'd forgotten how captivating she could be when she turned on the charm like that. "So now what?"

She took a deep breath, and he waited. "Well—and I know this sounds really strange, considering—I'd like us to be friends."

"Friends?" He nearly choked on the word. They may not have been very friendly lately, but they'd passed "friends" eight orgasms ago.

"I think it will be much easier as we go forward. We're going to be together for a very long time—um, I mean, the baby will always connect us, and it will be much easier for everyone if we're on good terms."

"I agree."

"Good." She blew out her breath and leaned her hips against the couch. "Wow. That was both harder and easier than I thought it would be. But I feel a whole lot better. Now, what were you going to say?"

"Something similar, actually." He was rewarded for his honesty by the look of surprise that sent Evie's eyebrows arching upward. "We certainly couldn't go on as we were."

"I'm *so* glad we got that sorted out." She rubbed her hands on her thighs and pushed to her feet. "And now, I'm suddenly very hungry. What about you? There's a wonderful Lebanese place not far—"

"There's one more thing we need to discuss, Evie."

"Oh. Okay." She resumed her earlier position, and braced her hands on the top of the couch. "What?"

"This." It was all the warning she got before he closed the distance between them and captured her mouth. Her gasp of surprise pulled air from his lungs. Then Evie melted into his embrace, her lips molding against his as her tongue slid greedily over his. Her hands roamed restlessly over his back before coming to rest at his waist, her thumbs hooking under the waistband of his jeans.

He'd meant the kiss as a simple demonstration—a reference for the point he was about to make—but desire soon took over, and he deepened the kiss as his hands slid up around her neck and into the mass of her hair.

He broke the kiss before he lost all control and hauled her into the bedroom, pressing his forehead against hers as he listened to her short, panting breaths.

"*This* is still an issue, Evie."

Her head was spinning now. "I think…." She had to pause to compose herself. "I think *this* crosses the line of 'friends.'"

"We can't ignore it."

Damn. He was devastating to her higher brain functions when he looked at her like that. *Think, Evie.* "But that doesn't mean we should explore it, either. Not immediately, at least."

"We're married, Evie. For the first time in your life, the people you're so worried about gossiping about you are actually expecting you to have sex. You should take advantage of that." Nick's hand slid around her waist, and the hurricane began to swirl.

"Marriage of convenience" was taking on a whole new meaning for her.

The dangers, though, of a marriage of convenience to Nick were quickly becoming clear. Nick's magnetism was almost irresistible, his eyes and voice hypnotic, but that feeling of serenity was sucking her in. Turning her on.

*This* was a perk, and as wrong as it seemed to build on it, it was a foundation of sorts. At least she and Nick had *something*.

But what happened in seven or eight months when she became too big and bulky and awkward to interest him? Was she signing up for even more misery later by not drawing a bold line in the sand now?

The hand around her waist tightened, and the pressure from his fingers increased, pulling her incrementally closer to him.

Her body was on board, practically screaming at her mind to quit thinking and just *do*. It was a foundation, and she reminded herself that she wasn't trying to build a foundation for forever. It wasn't the key to happily-ever-after, but it could be the key to happy-enough-for-now.

It would buy her some time so they could get to know each other better, find some common ground, and maybe, just maybe, change his opinion of her.

Even just a little. She'd settle for that.

Threading her fingers through Nick's belt loops, she tugged his hips to hers. Those dark eyes seemed to light from behind, and she was rewarded for her decision with a kiss that held wicked promises.

As far as "settling" went, she could settle for worse.

# CHAPTER TEN

*SETTLE* WAS RAPIDLY becoming her least favorite word in the English language. Two weeks after moving to Las Vegas, Evie had to bite her tongue every time someone said the word *settle* in her presence or else she might scream.

Gwen kept asking how she was *settling in*. Bennie wanted to know if she regretted *settling* for a quickie marriage. Will wanted to know if she'd *settled* all of her outstanding jobs and accounts before she left and how she was *settling* the ones she still had some activity in from Las Vegas. Her obstetrician promised her stomach would *settle* soon and recommended crackers and ginger ale for breakfast.

*Settle, schmettle.* It was a stupid-sounding word in the first place, Evie thought as she moved from a down dog into a plank position. *Settling* sounded passive, as if something would magically happen on its own, and she had no patience at this point for just waiting around for something to happen.

*Fortune favors the brave,* she thought, breathing in through her nose and lowering into a crocodile. Her arms trembled a little as she held the pose and counted under her breath. Dr. Banks had given yoga his stamp of approval at her first prenatal appointment yesterday, but she was now paying for the three weeks she'd taken off.

She couldn't claim to be brave, but she was certainly not

passive, either. Since she and Nick called their truce seventeen days ago, she'd plastered a smile on her face and jumped into her new life with great amounts of—however forced at times—enthusiasm.

Evie rocked her chest and hips forward to push through into an up dog and felt the stretch in her back. She held the pose and opened her eyes to enjoy the view. Nick's pool deck looked out over the desert's colors to the mountains in the distance. It was a far cry from the urban landscape she'd had from her windows the last ten years, and it had been a surprise to find that Nick didn't live among the lights of Las Vegas proper. She'd fallen in love with the view and spent as much time as possible out here in the shade of the awning, enjoying it. She almost hated to move back into down dog and lose the sight. Her calves protested, but she pulled her chest toward her thighs for a better stretch.

Yoga, like everything else, had to be done full-out whether she wanted to or not and regardless of how uncomfortable it was. But at least she was reaping results from that approach to her life.

She'd never be a perfect wife, but she was trying. Nick had a huge kitchen, and Evie discovered she really liked to cook. After some initial suspicion of her culinary talents and surprise that she not only planned to cook, but also claimed to enjoy it, Nick seemed pleased with her efforts and results.

The goal she'd set for herself sounded rather simple on the surface: try to get along. It wasn't as if she didn't have practice in that area. Years of Gwen's training provided her with a full set of skills designed for that, and Evie had had plenty of practice perfecting them.

After the first couple of days, it got easier, as she and Nick both kept to the unspoken terms of their cease-fire. Even though she could tell Nick still didn't quite like her, at least he didn't seem to actively *dis*like her, either. He was pleas-

KIMBERLY LANG                    137

ant—friendly, even, at times—and it was getting incremen-tally better every day.

Slim results were better than none, she kept reminding her-self. Hell, it was practically a mantra for her these days, and she repeated it as she moved into warrior two.

Her nights, though...

Her thigh trembled in a way that had nothing to do with the deep lunge. There were definitely perks in this arrange-ment, and sometimes, in the nonsense talk of afterglow, she felt as if she and Nick were coming to some kind of under-standing—she hesitated to use the word *relationship*—that just might be genuine and beyond the ground rules of peaceful coexistence.

*Work the bits you can....*

"Evie?"

She jumped and turned to find Lottie at the door. "Lottie! Is it eleven already?"

"I knocked, but there was no answer so I let myself in...." Lottie looked worried. "I didn't mean to interrupt."

"Please don't apologize. I'm glad you let yourself in. I just lost track of time. Can I get you something to drink?"

Lottie's unreserved acceptance of her had made Evie's transition much easier, and she was glad for the friendship. In many ways, Lottie reminded Evie of Bennie: practical and funny and straight to the point, only without Bennie's wild streak. Plus, Lottie was her husband's best friend's wife, and therefore a fount of information about Nick.

And Lottie's open personality meant Evie didn't have to pry for any details, either. Bonus.

But Lottie was Evie's savior today for an entirely differ-ent reason, and she sent Lottie to the sitting room while she got the snacks and drinks from the kitchen. When she returned with the tray, Lottie frowned at her slightly. "Are you sure about this? You don't have to."

"Believe me when I say I really *want* to. I did this all the time at home. Not to brag, but fundraising is something I'm pretty good at. That and PR. And y'all do so many great things, I'm just blown away."

Four days ago, when Lottie casually mentioned what the nonprofit center she worked for actually did and how they were trying to raise funds to rehab a community center in one of Las Vegas' poorest neighborhoods, Evie had pounced gratefully on the project.

"And you've saved me from going stir-crazy." While she *loved* the fact no one in Las Vegas knew her, and therefore had no expectations of her, not having anything at all to do had lost its luster after about four days. "I'm not used to not being busy and doing things, and the walls were already starting to close in."

Lottie looked around the spacious room and laughed. "You really do need something to do, don't you?" Picking up the pile of papers Evie had left on the table, she flipped through and whistled in appreciation. "When you do something, you go all out, that's for sure."

This wasn't park benches or the garden club; this was real effect on people's lives. Social-services counseling, after-school programs, drug and gang and teenage-pregnancy prevention—the Gleason Street Center provided it all. And, yes, Evie was fired up about it. Both HarCorp and the Harrison Family Charitable Trust had funding requests on the appropriate desk—Will's—already. The computer center and the basketball court were as good as done deals, but Lottie didn't know that yet.

"You have a very worthwhile project, and I'm just pleased you'll let me help." *Where was that spreadsheet?*

"I bet Nick's happy. What did he say when you told him?"

That got her attention. "I haven't mentioned it. Should I? Is Nick a donor already?" She frowned at that thought;

she'd planned to bring Nick on board later. Maybe with the library project…

Lottie choked on her drink. "You could say that."

When Lottie didn't elaborate, Evie knew she was missing an important piece to the puzzle. She leaned back into the corner of the couch and folded her legs under her. "Okay, spill. Give me all the details."

"Gleason Street is Nick's—and Kevin's—old turf. They both grew up not far from there. Did you not know that?"

Evie shook her head. "Nick told me he grew up in North Las Vegas, but since I didn't know the city, it didn't mean anything to me at the time."

And she'd forgotten until now. *Damn.* As part of preparing herself for this project, she'd spent some time researching the area, but she hadn't made the connection. The whole neighborhood was far below the poverty line; there were drugs and gangs… Evie chose her next words carefully. "Has the neighborhood changed much since then?"

"It's gotten a little better."

*Oh.* She knew Nick had earned his money and built his business with his own hands, but she hadn't realized his climb had been *that* steep. "They've come a long way, haven't they?"

Lottie nodded. "And they're proud of it. Nick actually uses it as a test on people sometimes."

"A test?" Alarm bells went off in her head. "How?"

"Oh, like when he meets people, he'll drop it into conversation to see how they react."

"Really?" Evie thought back to that first night. Nick *had* dropped that nugget of information before he knew she was from Dallas. She'd passed a test without knowing she was even taking it. No wonder Nick wasn't happy when he found out…

"If you think about it, it's a good way to cut to the chase with people. Especially the Old-Money types. Just because your daddy had money that doesn't make you any better than anyone else."

Evie's head snapped up, and she looked carefully to see if Lottie had directed that comment at her, specifically. But Lottie was still scanning printouts and budgets. That "you" must have been a general, nonspecific pronoun. "True. Money doesn't mean anything about a person's character."

"I know that, and you know that, but tell that to some folks." Lottie laughed, and Evie felt sick. Lottie obviously didn't know much about her background.

"Don't you think that's a bit of a broad generalization? Not all wealthy people are like that." Granted, Evie knew a lot who were, but not everyone with family money had a superiority complex.

"Precious few, Evie." Lottie's eyes grew wide as she read more of Evie's proposal. "Do you really think we could get some NBA players to come?"

Evie smiled weakly. "We can ask. The worst they can do is say no." Her stomach tied itself into a painful knot. "Still, you don't think testing people like that… I mean, it's a bit childish."

Lottie smirked. "Tell Nick that."

"I think I will, as a matter of fact." *One day.*

Lottie shrugged. "You can't really blame him, though, considering…"

"Considering what?" She wasn't sure she wanted to know at this point, but she *had* to ask.

Lottie looked at her wide-eyed. "Nick hasn't told you?"

*Would I be asking otherwise?* "Guess not, because I'm clueless."

"Well, it's probably not my place to go telling you…"

Evie tried hard to keep her voice light. "You have to now. I'm curious."

"Well, Nick's mother is—*was*—Farrahlee Grayson."

Evie wracked her brain but came up empty. Lottie must have been able to tell.

"I keep forgetting you're not from here. The Grayson family goes way back in Vegas. Not quite a 'founding family,' but definitely part of the boom years. There were even rumors that some of the family's money came from the mob, but that's neither here nor there. Either way, the Grayson family had bucket loads of money and they made sure everyone knew it."

The knots in her stomach were getting worse with each word. Evie knew she wasn't going to like this story at all, but glutton that she was, she had to hear it. And she probably couldn't stop Lottie now if she tried.

"So, Farrahlee's a bit of a rebel, and to tick her family off, she finds a guy her parents are guaranteed to hate and swears he's the one."

The alarm bells clanged with greater urgency. "Nick's father."

"Right. Gus. Farrahlee was just out for kicks, but she ended up pregnant. So, Gus and Farrahlee had to get married. I mean, you couldn't knock up Big Buddy Grayson's daughter and *not* marry her."

*Oh, dear Lord.*

"Farrahlee's father buys them a little house, gets Gus a good job and then cuts Farrahlee off without a dime. They last maybe a year or so after Nick was born before Farrahlee didn't want to play house anymore. She wanted her life, her money, her place as Big Buddy Grayson's daughter, back."

*This was not good....*

"Before Gus knew it, Farrahlee had divorced him, signed away parental rights to Nick and left the state. Gus went to Farrahlee's family, but they denied that they had any responsibility for Nick at all. Gus slowly began to drink himself to death at that point. He lost his job and the house and they ended up on Gleason Street. Nick had it rough. Really rough."

Evie sighed as the full meaning of the story landed in her chest like a rock. "Hence the chip on his shoulder."

"Exactly. His selfish, self-centered, stuck-up rich mother destroyed Gus's life and damn near destroyed Nick's. Evie, are you okay? You look pale."

She felt pale. "Just a little light-headed all of a sudden. I guess I didn't hydrate enough while I was out there in the heat."

Lottie, unaware that the world had just shifted, jumped topics. "I've always wanted to learn yoga. It seems like a good workout."

Evie dug deep into her bag of polite tricks. "And I'd love for you to come over sometime and exercise with me. It's a wonderful way to stretch." She tried to keep her voice at the same calm level, hiding her desperate curiosity. "So, where are Farrahlee and the rest of the Graysons now?"

Lottie shook her head as if it was a shame, but her voice belied the sentiment. "The family fell on hard times about ten or fifteen years ago. Big Buddy died about then, and they lost pretty much everything. Some folks had to leave town, some folks went to jail…. Farrahlee never came back to Vegas, and she died about five years ago. Nick was able to pick Starlight up for a song when they were selling off the last of the Grayson properties."

"A little comeuppance for the family?"

Lottie laughed. "Nick's whole existence—much less his success—is a big ol' poke in the eye for what few Graysons are still around."

Her nausea grew worse. "Success is the best revenge, they say. Nick's come a long way. And Kevin, too, obviously."

"They make a good team. I love him, but I don't know if Kevin would have had much drive to change his circumstances if Nick hadn't pushed him. He's not lazy or anything—he's just too laid-back to push too much."

"Kevin and Nick have known each other for a while?"

Which meant Kevin would share Nick's feelings toward Old Money, and therefore, *her*.

"Oh, they've been friends since they were like five or something. But Kevin's story is pretty much the same as half the kids' at Gleason Street—absent father, mother on drugs…"

"Would you excuse me for just a moment?" Without waiting for a reply, Evie stood and managed to walk calmly from the room. She closed the bathroom door and gripped the edge of the sink. He head was spinning, and she didn't quite know where to start processing the information Lottie so causally tossed her way.

She was horrified and indignant on Nick's behalf. His mother—hell, that whole family—was an insult to the decency of the human race. But, wow, it certainly explained a lot about why Nick didn't trust her, why he thought she would be a terrible mother…. Her shoulders dropped. Why Nick didn't like her much.

Because he thought she was just another Farrahlee. There were plenty of parallels, but still…

Talk about irony. Her life had plenty of examples of people who wanted to be her friend—or boyfriend—simply because she had money and came from the right family. Until now, she'd never faced anyone who didn't like her *because* of her family's wealth.

It wasn't as if she asked to be a Harrison. It was unfair of Nick to paint her as something simply because of her trust fund. It made her nauseous—like the morning sickness gone ten times worse.

It also made her want to kick Nick in a sensitive area. Who was he to accuse her of being shallow when he was the one passing judgment based solely on bank balances? That was a hell of a double standard.

Of course, the big question was now that she had new pieces to the puzzle, what was she going to *do* with them?

* * *

The volume of his stereo made him feel as if he had a teenager living in his house. Evie's musical tastes ran the spectrum from jazz to Top Forty, but the volume control only had one position: max. Granted, he tended to push the volume up a bit himself, but he'd spent too many years in bars and night-clubs where loud music and the subsequent slight hearing loss were expected. What was Evie's excuse?

He was getting used to coming home to the sound of music blaring, and, more recently, the smells of dinner coming from the kitchen. For the first couple of days after Evie moved in, she seemed uncomfortable with his house, but that had passed and she'd put her stamp on the place. Arrangements of fresh flowers graced tables. Art that had sat on the floor since the day he moved in now hung on the walls. She'd moved his fur-niture around and hired a different maid after finding the dust accumulated underneath.

After almost a year of living here, his house finally felt—for lack of a better word—homey. He had started looking for-ward to coming home, and a part of that, he wasn't ashamed to admit, was Evie.

He found her in the kitchen, her back to him as she stirred something on the stove, her head bobbing slightly with the beat of the music. She wore a simple cotton sundress with a low-cut back, and with her hair pulled up in a ponytail, he was treated to a lovely view of the elegant line of her neck and spine. She shifted her weight, leaning a hip against the counter and balancing one foot on top of the other.

Evie was barefoot. Pregnant. In the kitchen. He laughed out loud, and Evie dropped the spoon as she turned around.

"Nick! I didn't hear you come in."

"I'm not surprised."

Evie frowned as she slipped past him through the door, and a second later, the music volume dropped dramatically. When she came back in, she arched an eyebrow at him. "Are you sure you're only thirty-two?"

He arched an eyebrow back at her. "Are you sure you're really twenty-five?"

"If it's too loud, you're too old," she challenged as she opened the fridge, took out a beer and offered it to him. "How was your day?"

"Good. The sale on The Zoo went through."

"That's great. Congratulations."

"I'll keep it open for a little while, give the staff some notice, but I'd like to get started on the refurbishing soon."

Evie returned to stirring. "How sad. I'll miss those lighted vines. Hey, bring them home, and we'll hang them by the pool."

"Very funny." But he did like the way Evie referred to this as "home." "So what did you do today?"

"Picked up some paint samples for you to look at for the baby's room. Sent a resume to Circus Circus…"

"I told you I'd hire you if you wanted a job."

Evie shook her head. "Thanks, but after looking at the pitiful state of my resumé, I think I need to get some experience at places *not* owned by people I'm related to by blood or marriage." She paused and took a deep breath. "And I had lunch with Lottie."

Such a simple domestic scene: Evie puttering around in the kitchen while they discussed their respective days. It was almost as if they'd been doing it for years. And it hadn't been at all what he expected when Evie moved in. "Good. I'm glad you and Lottie are becoming friends."

Evie leaned against the counter and crossed her arms over her chest. "I'm going to be helping her with the Gleason Street Community Center project." She tossed it out like a challenge, but he wasn't sure why.

"I think that's great, Evie. You've certainly done a lot of fundraising and PR in the past." He chose his words carefully, wondering why she seemed so on guard about this. "I'm sure Lottie will appreciate your expertise."

"So I can count on you for a hefty check and ongoing support?"

*Was that sarcasm?* "Of course." When Evie didn't respond, he decided not to beat around the bush. "*What?* What's the problem?"

"Why didn't you tell me you grew up in that neighborhood?"

"I distinctly remember telling you that very thing."

She rolled her eyes. "And if I'd told you I grew up in Turtle Creek, would that have meant anything to you? Didn't think so. I'm from Dallas, how was I supposed to know what you meant by that?"

"Considering you were just on vacation, it didn't seem that important to elaborate."

"And now?"

"What do you want to know, Evie? I grew up in the projects. My dad was a drunk who couldn't keep a steady job. I didn't want to end up like him, so I worked my way through school, won a lot of seed money at the poker tables and bought Blue."

She smirked. "A true American success story. Making good through hard work, determination and luck."

Somehow, Evie made that sound like a slam. "I guess. And your point is?"

She sighed. "Nothing."

So much for that nice, homey feeling. "Go ahead. Spit it out."

Pushing out of her lean and wiping her hands on a towel, she shook her head. "You know, it's not worth it. I'm not going to pick a fight."

It was a little late for that, in his opinion.

Waving in the direction of the stove, she added, "Dinner will be ready in a few more minutes…."

"You brought this up, not me. If it's bothering you…"

Evie spun to face him. "Fine." With her hands on her hips, she met his eyes evenly. "What about those people who only needed luck? The luck to be born into the right family."

"Like you?"

She nodded. "That's one example, sure. It seems like the height of arrogance to assume those born into money aren't as appreciative of it or that they're somehow not as…as *good* as those who started with less."

"Evie, here's a news flash for you. Money doesn't always bring out the best in people."

"And poverty does?" Sarcasm dripped off the words. "No offense to your personal Bolshevik uprising, but money is nothing more than a tool. If that's the only tool in your tool-box, you'll never be happy. It'll warp your brain. Surely you've seen that."

"Spoken by someone who has a trust fund greater than the GDP of some small European countries. You lack credibility on this particular topic."

"And that huge chip on your shoulder makes you an expert on what, exactly? You know, a good therapist could help you work through some of these issues."

*What the…? "My* issues? Jesus, Evie, you're one to talk. You're not exactly the poster child of self-help and empow-erment."

Her chin went up. "But I'm not your mother, either."

He froze. "You don't know anything about Farrahlee Grayson," he said slowly, narrowing his eyes in warning and hoping she'd realize he didn't want to continue on that course of conversation.

No such luck. "Oh, I know enough. And while it doesn't make anything she did right or fair, I can see where having money and being Farrahlee Grayson was the identity she had and how losing that identity could have pushed her over the edge."

"You're defending her?" Three weeks ago he wouldn't have been surprised, but after everything recently...

"God, no. Not at all. The woman is an evil bitch and her whole family should be shot. Understanding *why* someone did something doesn't mean I sympathize or approve."

"You're assuming *I* don't understand why she left."

"Actually I think you *do*. And it's made you mad enough to live your entire life for the sole purpose of spiting her and her family. You're basically a good man with lots of potential, and you should be proud of your accomplishments. But you've got to let this go at some point."

Evie let her hands drop to her sides. "You've passed judgment on me, assuming I'm self-centered and selfish because of my bank balance." Her words were clipped, precise. "I'm actually relieved to find out that's where it's coming from, because my trust fund isn't me. I don't even know how much money you have, so I have to base my judgment of you on your actions. I think my judgment has a lot more creditability than yours."

"You're the one who showed up with a marriage proposal, a prenup and a divorce plan because you found yourself pregnant. Those actions just scream credibility."

She opened her mouth, paused and closed it with a snap before scrubbing her hands over her face and huffing. "Dinner's ready. Help yourself. I'm not hungry anymore."

She walked out of the room with her shoulders held back, but there was resignation in her step. A moment later, he heard a door close; not with a loud slam—just solid noise that spoke volumes.

He drained his beer, hoping the liquid would help cool his temper. Evie had made several valid points during her rant, telling him he that needed to reevaluate a few things. But *he* wasn't totally wrong, either, he reminded himself.

But if that were really the case, his conscience argued, why did *he* feel like the complete tool now?

# CHAPTER ELEVEN

EVIE DROPPED INTO THE ROCKING chair she'd purchased for this room with a groan of disgust at herself. Shooting off her mouth—and thereby shooting herself in the foot—had moved from being an occasional lapse to a full-time occupation.

*And things had been going so well.* Well, better, at least. The rocking chair she was currently sitting in was proof of her belief in that. And her hope. Why else would she be decorating a nursery unless she harbored the hope it would see good use?

Oh, she'd rationalized it, telling herself that Nick would want the baby to have a nice room of its own for when he or she came to visit. But now, as she berated herself for her astonishing inability to keep her trap shut, she had to admit that wasn't really the complete truth.

She'd been designing this room for the long term. It was a long-shot, secret hope—one she didn't really want to admit: the hope she and the baby might be here for much longer than originally planned. And that was totally stupid, considering the situation.

Because that meant… Well, damn. She shouldn't even go there. Crossing that bridge wasn't a good idea. Madness lay on the other side. As did heartbreak.

Evie leaned back and set the chair rocking, allowing the movement to calm her. Or trying to, at least. She heard the quiet knock a few minutes later and opened her eyes as Nick stuck his head around the door.

She searched his face carefully, examined his body language for clues to his mood and temper level. He seemed oddly…friendly? No, *friendly* wasn't the right description, but he wasn't openly hostile, either—amazing considering how she'd just blown her top and flounced out of the room in such a mature way.

"You like to get the last word, don't you? Make the dramatic exit?" Nick's mouth twitched in amusement, and Evie felt her muscles relax. He wasn't here to reopen hostilities.

Cautiously teasing, testing the waters, she tried for a small smile. "It's one way out of uncomfortable situations."

"Is it approved by your sister-in-law?"

"Oh, no. Flouncing—of any sort—is definitely not Miss Behavior-approved. It's a hard habit to break, though."

Nick crossed his arms and leaned against the wall. The silence stretched out, but it wasn't stretching her nerves. The energy in the room wasn't tense or angry. Nick wasn't mad, wasn't here to fight more, but the truce had been upended—thanks to her—and she got the feeling Nick was here to re-establish the treaty. And since she'd fired the first shot, she needed to extend the olive branch, as well.

She took a deep breath and swallowed her pride. "I'm sorry I blew up like that. I shouldn't have said—"

"Maybe those things needed to be said."

That was hope rising out of the ashes of her pride. "I lack finesse when I get angry, though."

"So do I."

*Fortune favors the brave.* She met Nick's eyes and made a cautious step out onto that bridge. "I'm not like her, you know."

Nick nodded. "I realize that. You're not the only one with bad habits, though."

It wasn't exactly a gushing declaration, but Evie grabbed

the hope it offered with both hands. Mentally steadying her-self, she edged another foot out on the bridge. "And I don't want to be like her, either." *There, she'd said it. She'd gone there. Sort of.*

Surprise registered on Nick's face, replaced a moment later by a slow, easy smile that made her insides melt. "History doesn't have to repeat itself."

Evie figured that was about as good as she could hope for at the moment and it was a good start. She put her feet down and stopped the rocker. "You know, I'm hungry after all."

Nick extended a hand to her and she took it. "Let's eat."

She took it, and with that, she was across that bridge and on the other side.

And it scared the hell out of her.

"Lord, you're such a butthead." Evie rolled her eyes at him as she made that pronouncement and flopped dramatically back onto the pillow. Then she ruined it with a giggle.

Nick pushed up on his elbow to face her. She was a vision: her hair all tangled and flowing across her pillow onto his and her cheeks flushed. "Did you really just call me a butthead? I haven't been called a butthead since third grade."

"Hey, I call 'em as I see 'em."

He picked up a lock of her hair and brushed it across her nose. "But you're not in third grade anymore. You can't come up with something better?"

"Other appropriate descriptions would not be very lady-like," she responded primly. Completely unselfconscious of her nudity, Evie looked like an exotic goddess—not a buttoned-up "lady" worried about appropriateness.

He used her hair to paint a line down the valley between her breasts before lazily circling a nipple and watching the shiver slide over her skin. "Is 'butthead' part of the Official Debutante Vocabulary?"

"It's not in the handbook, no, but—" Her forehead creased slightly, and she arched her back. "Ouch."

"You okay?"

She nodded as she sat up and rubbed at her lower back. "Muscle cramp."

"Roll over."

She grinned. "Again?"

Desire sliced through him. "Don't get cheeky. I'm offering to rub your back. However—" he let his eyes roam over her until she started to blush "—I'm certainly willing to rethink that offer."

"Back rub first." Evie flipped to her stomach and wrapped her arms around a pillow.

He knelt over her, straddling her hips, and savored the smooth warmth of her skin against his thighs. Gathering her silky hair in one hand, he lifted it out of the way and tucked it over her shoulder, leaving her back completely bare. He slid a finger down the indentation of her spine and watched goose-flesh rise. "Are you cold?"

"Not at all," she mumbled huskily, then cleared her throat. "Lower back, please."

Massaging slow circles at the base of her spine earned him an appreciative moan. His erection stirred to life, hardening against her backside.

"This is what I get for not exercising for three weeks. I knew I felt tight in my up dog this morning. It started bothering me a couple of hours ago." She shrugged, and he looked up to see her cheek move as she smiled. "I guess tonight's activities just aggravated—*damn.*"

His hands hadn't moved much; he couldn't be responsible for that pained curse. He quickly moved off her. "Evie?"

Evie rolled to her side and curled her legs up into her body, her arms wrapping around her waist. Her face had lost all its color, and her eyes squeezed closed in pain. A muscle in her jaw worked as she gritted her teeth and breathed in slowly through her nose. "Are you all—"

Fear—real fear like he hadn't felt since he was a child—slammed into him as Evie groaned again and pressed her hands against her stomach. His blood turned icy.

*The baby.*

Heart pounding, he scrambled for the phone.

Everyone was so kind. The doctors and nurses in the emergency room. The hospital volunteer who'd found her a set of scrubs to wear instead of her bloody clothes. The counselor who stopped by her little curtained-off bed in the E.R. to check on her and give her a card for a "recovery group." And especially Nick, who had worry lines etched into his stone face, but had sat by her bed while folks came and went and did all kinds of things to her—none of which stopped her from losing her baby.

They were all so damn *kind,* she'd wanted to hit something. And now, ten nightmarish hours later, she was still careening between that need and the need to lock herself in a dark room and bawl. But instead she had to sit here and listen to Dr. Banks talk about recovery time and coming back for a follow-up scan, when just two days ago, he'd been writing prescriptions for prenatal vitamins and pressing nutritional information pamphlets at her.

She'd taken so much for granted. It never occurred to her she wouldn't have this baby. And now she didn't. This had to be some kind of karmic payback for not wanting to be pregnant in the first place. The depth of the ache surprised her and killed her at the same time.

It was hard to focus on what Dr. Banks was telling her. "It's not uncommon to miscarry this early. It's nothing you did or didn't do." She should take comfort in that, but the wound was too fresh. "I can't find anything wrong with you physically, so there's no reason to assume you'll have any problems in the future conceiving or carrying a baby to term."

She opened her mouth, but Dr. Banks put a hand on her arm and squeezed gently. "It's not your fault." He turned to Nick. "Or yours, either. I'm so sorry about the baby, but you're perfectly healthy and these things really do just happen sometimes." She nodded because he seemed to expect it. "Now, do you have any questions for me?"

She did, but they all started with *why* and she already knew Dr. Banks didn't have any of those answers for her. No one did. She shook her head, which felt as hollow as the rest of her right now.

Dr. Banks had a kind face and a bedside manner that made her feel she could trust him at the same time it made her feel as if he really cared, but all that kindness and caring just rattled around in her hollow chest like marbles in a can. "I wrote you a prescription for some pain medicine if you need it over the next few days. Just rest and take it easy. And no sex for at least two weeks."

Out of the corner of her eye, she saw Nick's shoulders stiffen at the "no sex" edict. Did that mean he was upset it was off the cards, or insulted it even came up? And while she couldn't fault Nick's behavior or support through all this, he'd fallen into a silence that made his usual lack of communication seem positively chatty in comparison. He'd said all the right things at the right time, but none of them had *meant* anything. Nothing to let her know what he was feeling.

And then there was shaking of hands and patting of shoulders, and she and Nick were back in the car, headed home in silence.

Home. Where was that now? Nick's house? Not really; she was merely a guest there, just a step above an incubator for the baby. But home wasn't Dallas, either. She wasn't the same person she was even a couple of months ago, so she couldn't just go back and pick up her life where she'd left off. Her focus, her center, had shifted so dramatically recently, but that focus was gone now, and she was more than a little lost.

"How are you feeling?" Nick asked, breaking the quiet and causing her to jump.

What wasn't she feeling? Everything was all tied together, though, confusing her. "Tired."

He nodded. "Then you rest, and I'll go get your meds and something to eat."

He looked just as tired as she felt; there were shadows under his eyes, and she wondered if he'd slept at all in that plastic hospital chair. She'd had drugs—drugs that allowed her to sleep and escape the knowledge of what was happening for a little while.

There was something she should say—a lot she could say—but the words were trapped in her throat behind that backlog of conflicting emotions. "Thanks."

Nick followed her into the house "to help her get settled"— the word still grated across her nerves, but in a whole new way now—and she searched for words.

He stopped at the bedroom door, not following her in as she sat on the bed and toed off her shoes. She noticed the sheets were still tangled from last night's activities and askew from their hurried exit. She wanted to crawl under them and cry herself to sleep at the same time she didn't want to be there at all. As Nick turned around, she finally decided what she wanted to say. "I'm sorry."

His response was quick, but his voice was tired. "You heard the doctor—it wasn't anything you did or didn't do. It wasn't your fault."

"I can still be sorry." *For a lot of things.*

"Me, too." He was quiet for a moment, but he didn't meet her eyes. "But the doctor did say you would be able to have other children."

*You.* Not *we.* What had she expected? She lay down, the weight of everything just too much to bear any longer. "Yeah. He did say that. Maybe one day."

Nick looked in her direction—but not *at* her—a moment longer, the muscle in his jaw working, before he nodded. "Yeah. One day. I'll, um…I'll go get your meds."

He closed the door behind him as he left, and Evie burst into tears. Burying her head in the pillow that smelled like Nick only made her cry harder. She heard the crash, but couldn't bring herself to care enough to investigate.

She hadn't meant to get pregnant, but she did. And now she wasn't. She should feel relieved, but she didn't. Smelling his pillow made her think how happy she and Nick had been just hours ago, but she knew now that had been false. Just like their marriage license, it had been window dressing for the sake of the baby.

A baby she didn't have now.

She wrapped her arms around her stomach, berating herself for grieving so hard for something she'd barely had to begin with. But she couldn't help it. The baby hadn't been far from her thoughts simply because of the situation, but she hadn't realized that emotionally, at an elemental level, she'd connected to the baby and the idea of being a mother. Her rational brain hadn't really been focusing on *that,* but obviously something in her had. And now it hurt. Badly.

Following hard on that hurt—as if it wasn't enough or something—was the pain of knowing she'd lost everything. Her whole life—the new one she'd been working so hard to build—was crashing down around her. And she had no one to turn to.

She wanted Nick, but *that* wasn't what their relationship was about. How many times had he spelled that out to her? She'd just lost what their relationship was about, and Nick had just beaten a hasty path to the door. But that didn't seem to stop her from wanting him to be here with her now. She needed that. She needed him to talk to her, to tease her, to make her mad. Something. *Anything*.

Because otherwise, she had nothing.

In the car, Nick examined the blood on his knuckle. He didn't feel any better, and now he'd have to explain the hole in the drywall to Evie.

Provided she ever spoke to him again.

He'd never been so scared in his entire life. He'd known the baby was gone long before the doctors in the E.R. made their official pronouncements, but that pain had been held at bay as his real fear had centered on Evie.

She'd been whiter than the sheet on her hospital bed, but the blood... He hadn't expected that much blood. For a few minutes there at the beginning, he'd been sure she was going to die, but then her pain meds finally kicked in. It had been the longest time of his life.

But the worst had been—still was, actually—the hollow look in Evie's eyes that seemed as if she'd checked out mentally from the whole situation. He hadn't known what to say, and for the first time ever, Evie hadn't been very talkative. She hadn't needed him, and he hadn't been able to tell her... Well, anything.

So they'd sat there in silence. That silence had finally driven him to punching holes in the drywall in frustration and grief. The grief—he hadn't been prepared for that feeling.

This was his fault. No pregnant woman should have to deal with the level of stress he'd been putting on Evie. And he should have been more careful in general—Evie had said her research had said sex was perfectly safe, but hours of it? In multiple positions even the *Kama Sutra* didn't know? Had he once checked to make sure she was eating right? Resting enough?

At times, he'd almost forgotten the only reason she was

even there was because of the baby. He'd gotten used to having her around, started looking forward to coming home to her, and he'd forgotten this was a business arrangement.

And now their business was concluded. Once she recuperated from this, she'd want to go back to Dallas. Back to her life. What had she said last night—dear God, had it only been last night?—about Farrahlee wanting her identity back? Evie probably wanted hers back.

And while he could continue to hate his mother for her selfishness, he didn't blame Evie one bit. This situation was different, and it was only right for him to encourage Evie to do what she wanted. He owed her that much.

To prove it to her, he'd start by giving back some of the things she'd given up. Mikato's Sushi Bar was just a few more blocks. He'd get her sushi for lunch. And some regular coffee.

It was the least he could do. He didn't want to, but he owed her that much.

# CHAPTER TWELVE

THREE WEEKS. TWENTY-FOUR DAYS, if she wanted to be exact, since she'd given up hope, swept up the pieces of her heart and come home.

Evie lay on her couch and watched the ceiling fan turn, bored by the blur of the blades, but unwilling to find anything else to do. That would require energy, and it took all the energy she had just to get through each day, so she didn't have any to spare.

Physically, she was fine. Fully healed. Back to normal. No sign she'd ever been pregnant at all. And since she was fully caffeinated again these days, she had no reason to be so lethargic.

Mentally, she was a mess. Emotionally, she was a disaster area worthy of federal funding. She got up every day and put on a happy face, but she was simply going through the motions. "Evie Harrison" felt like a costume—an ill-fitting costume, at that—but the show had to go on. She didn't even feel as if it was her life anymore; instead, she felt as if she was the under-study, stepping in to fill a role that really didn't belong to her.

And she wasn't sure if she wanted to star in that show again, anyway.

She was safely back in the bosom of her family and friends and she didn't want to be here. She wanted to be in Vegas.

She wanted to be with Nick.

It had taken her a long time to admit that, because it was more pathetic than she could stand. In the days right after her miscarriage, Nick had been supportive and helpful, yet distant. He'd moved into the guest room without a word, and they became nothing more than polite roommates overnight. Then he'd started talking about Dallas as if it was the best place on earth, and she'd expected him to slap a plane ticket on the table at any moment.

As if it wasn't enough she lost the baby. She had to lose Nick, as well.

The double whammy on her heart had been more than she could take. She was trying to process and heal from two different, yet related, events. She could separate them in her mind to cope, and while she was starting to come to terms with the loss of the baby, the loss of Nick weighed her down like a sack of rocks.

After only a week, she couldn't take it any longer and she'd called HarCorp's pilot to come get her. Gwen arrived with the plane, and Evie had cried on her shoulder all the way home to Dallas. Though she never mentioned her pregnancy or her miscarriage, something in Gwen's eyes told her Gwen knew a lot more than she was letting on.

That was twenty-four days ago, and while she wasn't getting worse, she wasn't getting better, either. It seemed as if everything inside her had just shut down. She couldn't—*wouldn't*—cry anymore, but she wasn't bouncing back, either. Other than the constant pain in her soul, she felt...nothing. Bennie was threatening to send her to a therapist if she didn't "perk up" soon, but Evie didn't want to perk up. She wanted Nick, and since she couldn't have Nick, she wanted to wallow in the pain for a while longer.

*That* would teach her to fall in love with someone who didn't even like her, much less love her. The more painful the lesson was, the less likely she was to forget it.

And this hurt so bad....

The phone rang, and she wanted to ignore it, but she couldn't. *The show must go on.*

It was the doorman downstairs. "Mrs. Rocco…"

That was another knife in the chest. She wouldn't be Mrs. Rocco for much longer. And when *that* happened…she just prayed the numbness would continue so she wouldn't care what *Lifestyles* had to say about it.

"Yes, Howard?"

"Your brother is on his way up."

*Great.* Just what she did *not* need. "Thanks for the warning."

She swung her feet to the floor. The door was unlocked, but she couldn't be wallowing on the couch when Will arrived. She might as well make coffee.

A minute later, she heard the door open and Will was calling her name as he entered.

Evie forced herself to smile as she kissed his cheek. "Hey, Will, what brings you by?"

"I figured we should talk."

*Ugh. That's never good. Play ignorant.* "Okay. About what? Want some coffee?"

He shook his head at the offer and pinned her with a stare instead. "You haven't come back to work."

The truth would serve her well here, but it still needed to sound nonchalant. She shrugged. "Well, I think it's time I got a job on my own. Get out from under my brother's shadow for a while."

Will continued to stare at her. It made her a little nervous.

"And Kelley is doing such a great job—much better than I ever did—and it didn't seem right to give her a promotion and then take it away so quickly…." Still nothing from Will. *"What?"*

"Jackson tells me he's helping you file for a divorce."

"Remind me to talk to Jackson about what client confidentiality means," she muttered. "Yes, he is. I assumed you'd figured that out anyway when I moved back here. You were right. It was a stupid, impulsive thing to do." *And she was paying for it. Dearly.*

"But understandable under the circumstances," he said quietly.

*Did Will…* She searched his face carefully. *Damn it, he did.* "How'd you find out?"

A crease, so reminiscent of Nick's it cracked her heart, formed on his brow as he scowled. "I'm not stupid, Evie."

"Gwen told you, huh?"

Will didn't answer that. "*You* should have told me, Squirt."

The nickname brought tears to her eyes. "I thought y'all would be disappointed in me. Upset that I was about to embarrass the family again and give the gossips more to talk about."

"You worry too much about what other people think. I'm your brother, remember?" His voice softened a little. "And how are you feeling? Better?"

"I'm fine." She settled for a half-truth. "Early miscarriages don't have a lot of lingering effects."

He frowned again. "So why are you hiding in your apartment? You're practically a recluse."

*Argh.* "If you want me to present the checks and cut the ribbons for HarCorp again, I will. Just not yet, okay?"

Will lifted an eyebrow at her. "Evangeline…"

She held up a hand in weak protest. "Not now, Will. I don't want to fight with you."

The exasperation left his voice, and concern took its place. "Now I *know* something's very wrong with you. You've never backed down from anything in your life. Much less me."

"What?"

"Something's got you whipped."

*How dare he…* "I just had a miscarriage. I think I'm allowed to be whipped for a little while."

"No, I don't think that's it."

Anger prickled along her neck, causing her jaw to tighten. "How would you know anything? I didn't want to get pregnant, but I did. And I didn't know how much I wanted the baby until I lost it." Her voice cracked a little at the end. *I will not cry.*

Will crossed his arms over his chest and tried to stare her down. It was so irritating when he did that. "Then why aren't you in Las Vegas trying to have another one?"

A red haze clouded her vision, and blood pumped to her extremities. "You want to fight? Fine. Bite me, *William.*"

He didn't bite back. Instead he mocked her. "Or did you find out that Nick was a loser after all and now you're ashamed of the whole—"

*Son of a—* Her hand curled into a fist, her nails digging painfully into her palm, and she had to consciously release her fingers. "That's it," she snapped, her voice rising to a near shout. "How dare you come into *my* home and pass judgment on *anything,* much less my husband? You don't know squat about Nick or where he came from, or anything about *us* or our marriage, so just shut your mouth, you…" She trailed off as Will started to laugh. "What is so damn funny?"

Will's voice was warm as he reached out to touch her face. "There you are. I was afraid this guy really had damaged you in some way."

"So you picked a fight on purpose?" Will merely shrugged. "You like to live dangerously, don't you? No wonder Nick thinks my family is crazy." She flopped on the couch and rubbed her eyes. Will's plan had been dangerous, but it did shake her out of her funk and make her feel something beyond the pain and self-pity. That wasn't necessarily a good thing; too many emotions kept at bay for too long were now crowding in on her.

"We've been worried about you."

"We?"

"Gwen. Me." He sat next to her. "Gwen's been after me for a week now to go to Vegas and beat some sense into Nick—"

*Add flabbergasted to that list of emotions.* "Gwen? *Gwen* is on the warpath? Promoting violence?"

Very serious now, Will nodded. "And *I* was going to be next on her list if I didn't go rip Nick a new one."

Didn't she have a fifty on Nick in that fight? A hysterical giggle bubbled in her throat and she choked on it. "Will, *no.* Don't."

"I tried to remind her you were a Harrison and no one needed to fight your battles for you. Not even your big brother. I figured if you really wanted him, you'd go get him yourself. You didn't, though, and now that Jackson is serving papers on your behalf, I figured you didn't want him. But then you kept moping…"

"I'm not moping." Will snorted, and she rushed ahead. "I'm wallowing. There's a difference. Moping would involve ice cream."

"So you're 'wallowing.' Why?"

She couldn't seem to find her voice, and when she did, it came out small. Whipped. Pathetic. "Because I don't want a divorce."

She heard the sigh and waited for Will's patented exasperated-with-Evie tone. He didn't use it. "Then why are you here and not there?"

"Because Nick wants one." Saying that out loud hurt. "We only got married because I was pregnant, and now that I'm not…" She sighed. "My feelings changed. His didn't."

Will shifted uncomfortably. "If we're going to talk about boys and feelings now, maybe I should call Gwen. She's much better at that whole thing."

That made her laugh. "Just *a* boy. I thought for a little while he might be *the* boy. But he doesn't love me."

"Then he's stupid. And I thought we covered the whole you-dating-stupid-boys thing years ago."

This time, the laugh did make her feel better. "Thanks." She patted his leg. "Now you can get Gwen off your back without a trip to Las Vegas."

"I don't know. Sounds like Nick could use a good kick in the—"

"Very funny."

"You think I'm kidding?"

"I think it's best to let this go, no matter what I want. Nick and I have probably done enough damage to each other." She stood and blew out her breath. "I think I should file this away under 'painful lessons learned' and just go on like it never happened."

Will turned serious. "Good luck with that. Just don't wallow too much longer, okay?"

"Actually, I'm feeling a lot better now." Surprisingly enough, that wasn't a complete lie. "Wanna buy me dinner?"

"Sure, Squirt."

"Let me go freshen up. You can call Gwen and tell her I'm fine and she can put away the drums of war."

Will shook his head, but he had his phone out. She went to her bathroom to run a brush through her hair. Eying herself critically in the mirror, she realized she looked pale and a bit gaunt. No wonder Gwen and Will and Bennie were worried about her.

Her heart still hurt, but she didn't feel quite so hollow inside anymore. It was an improvement. She'd just have to settle for what she could get.

Ugh. She still hated that word.

Will had said that if she really wanted Nick, she'd have gone and gotten him by now. That's what Harrisons did, after all. He was only half-right. She wanted Nick, but she wanted him to want *her,* as well, and she couldn't swallow her pride enough to take that rejection again.

Painful lessons, indeed. There was no way she'd forget this one.

* * *

"Can I mention her name today, or will you bite my head off?" Lottie's head peeked around his office door as she asked the question.

"Mention who?" Nick laid the file he was reading on his desk. There was only one "her," but he was working hard to move on and outward appearances counted.

Lottie frowned. "Evie. Who else?"

His pulse accelerated, but he kept his voice even. "Of course you can mention her name. Why would I take your head off for it?"

"Kevin said…"

"Well, Kevin has really poor timing sometimes." In reality, Kevin was asking to get punched in the mouth for the way he kept talking about Evie, but he couldn't tell Lottie that.

"He did say she'd served you with divorce papers."

Kevin would be eating his teeth very soon. "She's not the first person in history to regret a quickie Vegas wedding."

Lottie's mouth twisted. "It seems so weird. Every time I saw her, she seemed so happy. And you guys really did seem like a good couple, right for each other somehow. I just don't understand." She shrugged. "I know, it's none of my business. I am sorry, by the way."

The knife that had permanent residence in his guts twisted a bit. "Is that why you brought her up? To tell me you're sorry we didn't work out?"

"No. I got something from Evie in today's mail that I wanted to ask you about."

"Evie's sending you letters?" *He* hadn't heard a word from Evie since she left for the airport. All communication had and would continue to be through her attorney.

"There was a note in there, thanking me for befriending her while she was here and inviting me to Dallas in the future. She's very polite, you know?"

"Her sister-in-law is some kind of manners guru. It's ingrained in her." And it must have rubbed off on him, otherwise he'd have stopped this conversation long before now. "So what else did she send you?" he prompted.

"Checks. Big, fat, massive checks for the Gleason Street Community Center."

He didn't need to hide his surprise. "Checks, plural?"

"One from something called HarCorp…"

"That's her family's company," he supplied.

"One from the Harrison Family Charitable Trust, and one from her personal account. There's a lot of zeros involved."

That he didn't doubt at all. "Evie can afford it. The checks will cash, don't worry about that."

"I'm not. I'm just wondering why she'd still bother. I mean, now that she's gone back to Texas."

"She likes giving money to projects that make a difference in people's lives. And she told you she'd help with the fundraising. Since she's not here anymore, I assume this is how she's fulfilling that promise." *Salving her conscience, maybe?* "Cash the checks and move on."

"If I cash these checks, we're going to have to name a wing of the building after her."

Now he knew why Lottie was so cautious about this. "That many zeros, huh?"

"*That* many zeros."

*Good Lord.* "Cash them." Something good could come of this debacle. He picked up the file he'd been looking at earlier, and Lottie took the hint to leave.

But Nick couldn't regain his earlier focus. Evie couldn't do *anything* halfway, could she? She got pregnant, so she had to get married. And she couldn't just get married; she had to move to Las Vegas. Into his house. Into his life. Into his heart.

He shook that thought off. The divorce papers delivered to him were an unwelcome reminder of how badly out of hand this whole situation had gotten because Evie couldn't go just halfway.

Well, she'd gone halfway on *one* thing. She hadn't fallen in love with him. Which sucked for him, since it was the one thing where he *had* gone all the way.

So he'd stalled on signing the divorce papers, when he should have just done it immediately and moved on. Prenups certainly made the divorce proceedings much quicker—if not easier.

Of course, when had anything with Evie been easy? From that first night, when his car had been broken into, up to now, *nothing* had been easy when it came to Evie. His whole life had been turned upside down.

And to prove how sick the whole situation really was, he actually *missed* it. Life seemed a little boring now without Evie and never knowing what she would throw at him next. He had learned a lot about himself recently, including a tendency toward masochism he didn't know he had in him. Why else would he want a woman so desperately when she did nothing but drive him crazy?

He even missed fighting with her—the snap and fire in her eyes, the way her skin turned pinker as her temper flared, how she could channel that heat in a completely different direction in a heartbeat. They fought, sure, but they fought fair and Evie never held a grudge. She had a short fuse and a big temper in that sinful body, and she was a yeller.

In more ways than one, he thought as a familiar heat spread over his skin like a painful memory.

Good thing he wasn't, or else every fight would have been a recreation of Evie and Will going toe-to-toe on the balcony, only with him playing her brother's role. Common sense should tell him this divorce was the right thing to do, because no relationship could handle *that* level...

He stopped that line of thought, confused. For all that yelling he witnessed, Evie and her brother were very close.

Tight, even. Even when Evie complained about him—which was frequently—there was no doubt she loved her brother. And Will, for all his glowering, seemed to adore her—even when she yelled at him.

He could relate to *that*. Adoring Evie, at least.

Evie *had* said that he reminded her of Will. Even called him the same epithet…

A thousand details hit him at once, and it led to clarity. Evie being so polite and gracious to everyone even though he knew it grated across her nerves at times. Evie guarding her tongue so she didn't end up in the papers. How she talked about "Evangeline Harrison" sometimes as if it was a different person.

That constant pressure had to build until it blew, and Evie was safe exploding at her brother. Because she loved her brother. Trusted him. Felt safe just being Evie.

Amateur armchair psychology was new for him—he didn't consider himself one for plumbing the depths of anyone's psyche—but this just might make sense. Did Evie only shout at the ones she loved?

Did that mean she might have feelings for *him?* Or was that just wishful thinking?

If she did, why did she leave without a fight? *Because I was very clear why I married her.* And he hadn't given her much reason to question that as circumstances changed.

Oh, he was an idiot, and he'd screwed up big time. He was a day late and a dollar short in this hellish mess. His wife had planned their divorce the day she married him, but now that she had moved to a different state and served him with divorce papers, all bets were off and he wanted to change the game.

He looked at the divorce papers and smiled. He happened to be quite good at games of chance. He'd anted up, and it was time to call her bluff and play the cards.

This was going to be interesting.

# CHAPTER THIRTEEN

After surprising society—and her family, too, if reports are to be believed—with news of her nuptials and then disappearing for several weeks, Evangeline Harrison, now Rocco, is back in town, *sans* her new husband. While Dallas is glad to have her back, Evangeline is keeping a low profile these days, and hasn't been seen in society much, nor has she returned to her former position at HarCorp. This, of course, has led to much speculation about the situation. Is the honeymoon over? Is Evangeline back for good or only a visit? And where is her husband, Las Vegas nightclub owner Nick Rocco?

"IN LAS VEGAS, YOU NOSY witch," Evie answered with a scowl as she tossed today's issue of *Dallas Lifestyles* into the recycling bin. "Not that it's any of your damn business," she added as she closed the lid with a satisfying bang.

After much consulting with Gwen over shoe shopping and lattes, Evie knew there was no way she was going to be able to spin her divorce to make it less interesting for the gossip-hounds. Not if her intentionally low-key return to town was already newsworthy of speculation.

She breathed the steam of her coffee deep into her lungs

as she leaned against the kitchen counter. *Hello, my life. How I* haven't *missed you at all.*

Of course, she would have to announce soon enough that she was getting divorced—those records would be public information once they were officially filed with the judge—and she knew the importance of preempting news like that. Not that she really cared anymore what people said about her. She was going through the motions out of habit more than anything else.

If she could manage to keep this under the radar, great. But she wasn't stressing over it, either.

The stress came from simply waiting. So far, there'd been no word from Nick or his attorney all week, so there was nothing to preempt for the gossips.

She still jumped every time the phone rang, both anticipating and dreading the call from Jackson that would end the suspense, but the limbo was killing her a little more each day. If Nick didn't make a move soon, she'd have to do *something* to break this stalemate. She couldn't go on like this. Nick haunted her dreams, even though she spent her days trying not to think about him or what life might have offered if things had worked out differently.

But she wasn't planning a return to her old life, either. Hell, she wasn't even sure how much longer she'd stay in Dallas. There wasn't *that* much keeping her here beyond her family, and she'd already reconciled herself to being away from them when she moved to Las Vegas. The offer of an interview from Circus Circus based on the resumé she'd sent had been a wake-up call, spurring her realization that she didn't have to stay in Dallas and be what everyone expected her to be. There was a whole world out there waiting to be conquered.

She'd turned down Circus Circus because Las Vegas—while tempting—wasn't on her short list of possible places.

California. New York. Chicago. Maybe even London. The choices were endless. But she couldn't explore *any* of those possibilities until she heard from Nick. Nick's *attorney,* she corrected herself.

And she had no idea when that would be.

She needed to finish getting ready. She and Gwen were going shopping this afternoon for the boys' birthday, and the symphony fundraiser was tonight. Without a good excuse, Evie needed to be there or else give everyone more fodder for *Lifestyles.*

Leaving her mug in the sink, she pushed through the swinging door, heading for her bedroom. As she passed through the living room, she heard the door *snick* as the knob turned and the lock tongue moved out of the frame. Stepping back toward the kitchen, where she'd left her phone, she mentally ran down the list of possibilities.... Will was at work; Bennie was at the beach; Gwen was meeting her at the mall. Anyway, the front desk would have called if she had a guest.... No one should be entering her apartment right now, and adrenaline rushed through her veins as the door started to open.

She was taking a deep breath to scream as a man stepped through the open door.

The scream died in her throat. *Nick.*

Her knees wobbled, and she couldn't say if it was from the adrenaline rush or the fact he looked so good she wanted to cry. Her heart still beat frantically in her chest, but that could be caused by either situation, as well.

"Evie? You look pale."

"Because you scared the living daylights out of me barging in like that. Don't you knock?"

"I did. No one answered."

"I was in the kitchen." *Driving myself insane thinking about you.*

Nick shook his head at her like a scold. "I told you not to leave your door unlocked. Anyone could just walk right in."

"I live in a manned building on a secured floor for a *reason.*

No one can just walk in here unless they live here." She stopped. "How'd you get in, anyway? No one at the desk called up."

"Howard and the gang don't seem aware that you filed for divorce. They just waved at me as I passed." He looked at her hands and frowned. "You're not wearing your ring, though."

She tugged the chain out of her shirt, letting the band dangle in front of her. "I wear it when I go out." It had been too painful to wear it on her finger, but it hurt to take it off altogether. "It seemed premature to quit wearing a ring when you hadn't signed the papers. It could lead to questions I don't want to answer." *And it would make it all real. Final.*

Nick cocked his head and looked as if she was an oddity in a sideshow. "So you haven't told people yet?"

This was embarrassing—to be caught like this. And she was completely unprepared to *talk* to Nick. Her stomach was turning over itself, and she didn't feel steady on her feet. "Just my family. And they know everything now, by the way. Well, Gwen and Will do, at least. I didn't see the sense in upsetting Uncle Marcus more than he already is by mentioning the baby."

"How are you feeling?"

*Miserable.* "I'm fine." *Pull your act together. You can get through this.* The muscles in her cheeks protested as she stretched them into a smile and tried to channel Gwen's calm coolness. "Perfectly healthy and back to normal. Thank you for asking. Would you like a seat? Something to drink? Coffee?" She was proud of herself; her voice didn't shake or crack, and this was very civilized.

She thought she saw Nick's mouth twitch briefly, but it must have been a trick of the light or her own scattered brain messing with her. "I'll sit, but nothing to drink, thank you."

Nick took one of the chairs, so she chose the opposite one to maximize the distance between them. She knew better than to get too close to him. Her dreams had been too vivid recently to risk proximity. *Be friendly and polite.* "So what brings you to Dallas?"

"You."

Her heart stuttered. "Me?" she squeaked. *So much for that earlier pride.* She cleared her throat.

"There's a problem with the papers you sent. I can't sign them."

Her heart soared. "Really? Why?"

"Nevada is a community-property state."

And now it crashed and burned. "Oh." She tried to keep the disappointment out of her voice. "But that shouldn't be a problem. We weren't married long enough to acquire anything."

"Technically, I bought The Zoo *after* we got married. That's community property now, and there's residency issues, plus the waiting period...."

Her head was spinning. "Jackson said..."

"Maybe Jackson isn't as up-to-date on Nevada law as he should be."

Surely Jackson looked into all of that... "The Zoo isn't a problem. I don't want it. I mean, I don't expect you to divide it. I'll sign off my share or sell it to you...."

Nick's eyes widened. "You want me to *buy* my own club from you?"

"I *said,* I'll just give it to you, but if that's not possible I'll sell it to you for a dollar or something...." Her disappointment over this "reunion" was quickly turning to frustration and confusion.

"And your prenup? That's a problem, too."

That jerked her back to the conversation. "What? The prenup? What are you...?" Nick wanted money from her? She stopped and took a deep breath. "Look. If there's a problem with anything, your lawyer can contact Jackson. I'm sure they can work around whatever the problems—"

"You can't just work around the law."

Evie felt her temper rising and fought to keep a lid on it.

"That's *not* what I'm saying. I'm just trying to get us out of this disaster with minimal damages to either of us. I don't want *anything* from you. Not money. Not your club. Nothing. An uncontested divorce shouldn't be this much trouble."

Nick nodded. "But my attorney has informed me that I have grounds for divorce, and that changes everything."

"What grounds?"

"Desertion."

*What the…?* "I didn't desert you."

Nick raised an eyebrow and indicated the room. "Looks like it to me. It'll probably look that way to the judge, too. That cracks that 'iron-clad' prenup of yours."

*Now she was mad.* "Son of a—"

"Language, Evie," Nick scolded. "Name-calling is not appropriate behavior for a lady."

That sent her to her feet, her blood boiling. "Don't try that with me. If you're spoiling for fight, bring it on."

Evie was mad. *Good.* It certainly beat that uncertain look from earlier that had led her to hide behind all that false politeness. He'd risked a lot, pushing her like that, but Nick was gambling here, and when the stakes were high, he knew he had to take the risks.

Of course, now Evie looked as if she'd like to remove his head from his body. "Big ugly battles end up in the papers. You sure you want that?"

Her chin went up a notch. "I don't care what people think anymore. I'm tired of living my life like that."

*Good for her.* "And your family?"

"Love me unconditionally. That knowledge…that's the one good thing to come out of this nightmare."

"At least *you* got something for your trouble, right?"

Eyes snapping, she turned on him. "Is *that* what this is about? You want something for *your* trouble?"

"You were the only trouble I had."

Instead of firing back, Evie seemed to deflate. She sighed and her shoulders dropped. "Yeah. I know. I've brought nothing but trouble to myself and everyone I love with this whole situation."

*Did she include him in that group?*

"I owe you an apology, Nick. For everything."

He hadn't been expecting that. "Such as?"

"I panicked, and I shouldn't have. I put you in a bad position and then did nothing but exacerbate it. I have a bad temper, and I tend to jump into things with both feet without thinking it all the way through. So I'm sorry about everything I put you through. Including the mess I seem to have made of our divorce." She shook her head sadly and a bitter laugh escaped. "After the mess I made of our marriage, I don't know why I'm surprised I messed this up. I certainly don't want part of The Zoo or any of that. If you'd like a cash settlement for your trouble, I'll talk to Jackson and have him work that out with you and your lawyer. You deserve at least that much."

What he deserved and what he wanted were two completely different things. He didn't deserve much of anything, but he *wanted* a hell of a lot. "That was quite a speech. When you decide to humble yourself, you certainly go all the way."

"It's not false humility. I can admit to my mistakes."

He wasn't sure he liked her tone. "And marrying me was a mistake?"

She smiled weakly. "I think we've proven that beyond a shadow of a doubt. I know money won't fix anything, but that's really all I have to offer."

She had a lot to offer him, but she didn't know that. "I didn't realize being married to me was such a burden that you'd be willing to *pay* to get out of it." Maybe he'd read this whole situation wrong. She certainly seemed resigned to her choice and determined to get it done as quickly as possible. He'd come to call her bluff; he'd never considered she might not be bluffing after all.

Evie ran her hands over her face and through her hair. "Being with you is many things. *Burden* isn't the word I'd choose." Then she turned to him and sighed. "It's definitely been an adventure. An eye-opening adventure for me, and though I know it has sucked for you, I'm actually very appreciative for that."

"Did I ever say it sucked for me?"

"You didn't have to." Her mouth twisted as she said it and he felt like that first-class bastard. "I'm sorry it turned out this way, but I would like to at least part as friends."

It had taken everything she had to get that speech out of her mouth, but she'd been careening from one emotion to the next and she just didn't have anything left in her.

Nick's eyes narrowed. "I don't think we can be friends."

Considering what she really wanted, hearing Nick say that was about the last blow her heart could take. "I'm sorry to hear that. I'll take you off my Christmas-card list."

"That's it? You just roll over? What's happened to you? Where's the Evie that charges in and goes for what she wants? The Evie who was willing to take me on over anything and everything?"

"She's tired of fighting. Look, I'm smart enough to know when I can't have what I want, and it's time to give up this fight."

There was that sideshow oddity look again. "Tell me the truth, Evie. What do you want?"

*You.* But she couldn't say that. "It doesn't matter."

"I think it does."

"Do you know what *you* want, Nick?"

"Yeah, I do."

"What's that?" When he hesitated, she tried to sweeten the

offer. "I just need this to be over with, so whatever it is, tell me, and if it's within my power, I'll happily give it to you."

Nick broke eye contact as he thought, and she knew she should be worried what he was going to ask for if it required that much thought. She'd put herself in a place of weakness for this negotiation, but she just needed this over with. Her heart couldn't break into any more pieces without killing her for real.

"I just want to ask you something."

"Okay."

"Were you happy in Las Vegas? At any time?"

It was an odd question, but she could answer it without hesitation. "Yeah, I was. Most of the time," she acknowledged.

"With me?"

"I know it sounds hard to believe, but I was—when I didn't want to strangle you, of course." He smiled, and that gave her a little courage. "Honestly, I thought for a little while there that we might be able to make it work. But we got married for all the wrong reasons, and it was just too much to overcome. Had I known the divorce would be this complicated, I wouldn't have asked you to marry me in the first place."

"There's actually a very simple solution to this divorce situation."

"Really?" She tried to inject some enthusiasm into her voice. "Tell me."

"We don't get one."

Her jaw fell open, and she couldn't manage to close it. It felt as if sunshine was pouring into the dark hollows of her chest, and her heart started to beat for the first time in ages. She stomped down the feelings; there was no way she heard that correctly. "I'm not following you."

Nick rubbed his palms against his thighs. "You're not making this easy on me. I've tried every way I can think of—including getting you mad at me—to break down that wall you're hiding behind." He laughed. "I should know better by now. So, I'm just going to have to bite the bullet."

She was teetering on a knifepoint, unsure if she should be hoping or praying. She swallowed hard and braced herself. "Um…okay."

"I don't want a divorce. There. I said it. I don't want a divorce, and I want you to come home. To Vegas."

That sunshine seemed to pump through her veins, filling her with hope. It was *cautious* hope, but without clarification… "Home? With you?"

Nick rolled his eyes in exasperation. "No, with Siegfried and Roy and the tigers. Of *course* with me. Jesus, Evie, how difficult are you going to make this for me?"

"But…"

Nick stepped closer to where she sat. "Do you really want a divorce? You just said you thought we might be able to make this work. Don't you want to try?"

She stood and crossed the room, not wanting Nick to get too close. She needed space—to think, to breathe. "What I *need* is to just get over you. And that's proving difficult enough—"

Nick interrupted her with a half grin. "Get over me? That rather implies…"

*Me and my big mouth.* "All right. Fine. You win." Nick just looked at her expectantly. "Do I really have to say it?"

Nick nodded and stood there, seeming to enjoy watching her die of embarrassment.

She crossed her arms over her chest and squared her shoulders. "I don't want a divorce, either, okay? For some reason known only to God and it's probably proof I'm truly insane, I'm in love with you." Nick's grin grew and she wanted to smack him. "I'm sure a good therapist will be able to help me sort this out."

Nick stalked toward her and she backed up a step. And then another.

"I'm probably confusing good sex with love or maybe all those pregnancy hormones messed my head up. Or something like that." Oh, *no;* she'd backed herself into a corner, and Nick closed in on her as she put her hands out to block his approach. "Um, Nick, I—"

He cut her off with a kiss. It was both sweet and hungry, sending happy shivers all the way to her toes at the same time it sparked her nerve endings to life. Nick leaned in, pressing his chest against her palms, and she could feel the heavy thump of his heart as it kicked up speed and he deepened the kiss.

She relaxed her hands and let them slide up his chest to his shoulders and finally clasp around his neck. Rubbing her thumbs against the muscles there, she heard his sigh as he broke the kiss and moved to nuzzle her temple.

"Missed you," he murmured against her hair.

"And…?" she prompted. Instead of answering, Nick's lips moved to her earlobe. She shivered, but she wouldn't be distracted by that. "Don't leave me out here on this ledge alone."

Nick pulled his head back and tilted her face up to his. "And I love you."

Peace settled on her shoulders, lightening her heart. "I've missed you, too."

"So you'll come home with me?"

She nodded, then gasped as Nick lifted her off her feet. Did he mean this very second? But no, the bedroom was the destination, and she wanted to shout with happiness when she saw the look in his eyes as he pressed her onto the mattress and lay at her side.

Propped on his elbow, he loomed over her, one hand tracing a lazy path up from her hip, over her waist and rib cage before stopping in her cleavage where her ring was nestled. Nick's eyes darkened again as he slid a finger over the thin gold chain. Then his fist closed around the ring, and one quick tug broke the chain.

He slid the ring back where it belonged with a tenderness that made her heart melt. "Much better," he told her. Then he frowned. "But still not right."

"Why? What's the problem?" She examined the ring, looking for a flaw.

"You need a rock. Some big, fancy bling to show off at your country club. And if we're going to do that, you might as well do the whole big white wedding thing. Give the paper that princess wedding they expected." Nick's fingers were working on the buttons of her blouse as he spoke, and a moment later it was on the floor.

"We can't do th-that." She stuttered when his mouth moved along the lace edge of her bra.

"Why not?" Now he was working the clasp of her jeans.

"It's against the r-rules. You only get one wedding. A do-over is tacky." He looked up at her, and she added, "Trust me on this. I know what I'm talking about. Gwen would have a cow…." She sat straight up as she remembered. "Oh, no! I'm supposed to meet Gwen."

*"Now?"* The disappointment in his voice amused her and aroused her at the same time.

"We were supposed to go shopping. Just don't move." She scrambled for the phone. "Let me call her and tell her… What *am* I going to tell her?"

Nick tugged on her arm, pulling her back onto the bed. "That you're very busy at the moment." He hooked his thumbs in the waistband of her jeans and panties and slid them down over her legs. Then he grinned wickedly at her. "And naked."

Fingers shaking from the kisses Nick placed on her inner thigh and the wet heat of his tongue moving against her, Evie barely managed to text Gwen with a message cancelling shopping. Whether it made any sense or not, she didn't know, and she didn't care as she dropped the phone and arched against Nick's mouth with a groan.

When she could think again, she tugged at his hair, pulling him up until they were eye level. "You are so bad."

"And here I thought I was pretty good." One quick thrust of his hips, and, *thank heaven,* he was buried inside her. "I can always try again and see if I can do better."

She was already trying to find a rhythm, rocking her hips against his. "Later."

Nick dropped his forehead to hers and held still. "Marry me, Evie. Again."

"I told you, it's tacky," she gasped, her fingers digging into his arms. She was going to die soon from wanting. "*Please,* Nick."

"I'm from Vegas. We invented tacky." He moved his hips just enough to send a shock wave through her. "Marry me."

She met his eyes. "Tell me you love me."

With a seriousness that healed every crack in her heart, Nick cupped her face and whispered, "I love you, Evangeline Rocco."

"Then I'll marry you. Again." She wanted to say more, but Nick was moving and she couldn't hold a thought in her head.

Two hours later, Nick asked, "Where do you want to go for our honeymoon?"

She thought for a minute. Just a few hours ago, she'd been examining all kinds of potential places to go. None of them seemed very tempting now, and Las Vegas, which hadn't even made her short list earlier, was the only place remotely interesting at the moment.

While Nick expressed surprise, it made perfect sense to her. After all, she'd gotten very, *very* lucky in Vegas.

# EPILOGUE

EVIE GROWLED LOW IN HER THROAT as pain creased her sweaty brow. He couldn't tell if she was growling at the actual pain or simply because she was in pain at all.

Nick smoothed her hair back from her forehead, only to have that growl redirected at him.

"Do not touch me," Evie gritted out. "This is all your fault, and you're not to touch me again as long as you live." She groaned and gripped the steel rails of the hospital bed. "And that might not be for too much longer," she snarled.

Sunny, the labor and delivery nurse whose attitude matched her name, patted his shoulder. "That's just the pain talking. She doesn't mean it."

He hesitated correcting her. Evie didn't make empty threats, and she was probably plotting his demise—his painful demise—during the moments of calm between contractions. Those moments were getting shorter, though, and he was feeling bad enough at this point to accept whatever painful torture Evie had in mind. She was in so much pain… "Can't you give her something? Anything?"

Sunny shook her head. "Not at this point. But we're getting close."

Another contraction gripped Evie, and his wife seemed to

channel that kid from *The Exorcist*. "This can't be normal," he complained.

"Evie didn't plan on doing this naturally, so she wasn't prepared for the pain. That's making it worse for her." Sunny checked a monitor and murmured encouraging words to Evie.

With the next contraction, Evie cursed a blue streak and threatened to remove a part of his anatomy she'd been rather fond of until her water broke.

"Language, Evie. You're going to be someone's mother." Will's dry tone contrasted with the lines etched on his face. Will was handling this only slightly better than Nick was.

"Bite me, Will. I don't know why Gwen didn't kill you after the twins were born."

"Because Gwen—unlike *some* people—was smart enough to get to the hospital before the window for her epidural closed."

"I was busy," she panted, "you butthead—" *pant, pant* "—how was I supposed to know…"

As Evie and Will bickered, Sunny frowned. She motioned him closer. "Do I need to get her brother out of here?"

"No. They're always like this. It's probably good for her—taking her mind off the contractions." And as long as Evie was sniping at Will, he himself wasn't in her crosshairs. Will had planned to come closer to Evie's due date anyway, so it was a nice coincidence he'd been in town for the dedication of the new Harrison-funded day-care center at Gleason Street when Evie went into labor two weeks earlier than expected. Gwen was still en route.

They'd waited over a year before trying to get pregnant again, and Evie had received the news they were successful with cautious optimism, unconvinced she wouldn't miscarry again and too scared to get her hopes up until after they crossed the three-month mark. After that milestone, Evie's entire outlook changed, and she'd become almost Madonna-like in her serenity during this last trimester. That had been a bit of a shock, but the feisty Evie he knew and loved was back now. With a vengeance.

Dr. Banks pushed through the door, his white coat flapping behind him. "Are you ready to do this, Evie?"

Evie smiled angelically at her doctor, relief written all over her face. "Yes. *Please.*"

"Then let's have a baby." Dr. Banks motioned to Will, who squeezed Evie's hand on his way out, and Sunny directed Nick into position as she helped Evie sit up.

Evie met his eyes then. "Wipe that smile off your face. I'm holding you *personally* responsible for this."

"The baby's crowning. Push, Evie!"

She squeezed his hand and smiled. "Thanks."

*From page three of Dallas Lifestyles:*

Evangeline Rocco, née Harrison, was spotted shopping with our own Miss Behavior and Sabine Wyndham last Saturday, while baby Charlotte spent the day with her doting father, Las Vegas nightclub magnate Nick Rocco, uncle, HarCorp's Will Harrison, and cousins in the HarCorp skybox watching the Rangers game. The newest addition to the Harrison-Rocco family empire then made her Dallas debut Sunday morning at St. Matthew's Cathedral in a beautiful hand-stitched christening gown reportedly imported from France for the occasion. No official photos of baby Charlotte have been released by the family yet, but casual snaps are surfacing as Evangeline introduces her daughter to the sights and society of her hometown.

Dallas society has suffered greatly from the loss of Evangeline to the lights of Las Vegas, but all reports indicate our Evangeline has taken Sin City by storm, as well....

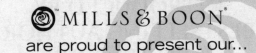

# MILLS & BOON®

## are proud to present our...

# Book of the Month

## The Baby Gift
### A beautiful linked duet
### by Alison Roberts from
### Mills & Boon® Medical™

### WISHING FOR A MIRACLE

Mac MacCulloch and Julia Bennett make the perfect team. But Julia knows she must protect her heart – especially as she can't have children. She's stopped wishing for a miracle, but Mac's wish is standing right in front of him – Julia...and whatever the future may hold.

### THE MARRY-ME WISH

Paediatric surgeon Anne Bennett is carrying her sister's twins for her when she bumps into ex-love Dr David Earnshaw! When the babies are born, learning to live without them is harder than Anne ever expected – and she discovers that she needs David more than ever...

Mills & Boon® Medical™
Available 6th August

Something to say about our
Book of the Month?
Tell us what you think!
millsandboon.co.uk/community

# Secrets. Lies. Time to come clean…

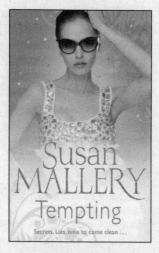

Dani Buchanan is horrified when her father turns out to be a presidential candidate. And then the tabloids find out…

Katherine Canfield is unable to bear children. Dani's a reminder of what Senator Canfield could have had – and Katherine's jealous.

Adopted Canfield son Alex is tempted by Dani. With the scandal of the century brewing, can he pursue a relationship that could tear his family apart?

## Available 3rd September 2010

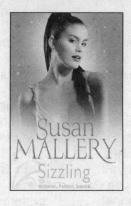